WHITE AND LICKED CLEAN

He started down. The steps turned a sharp corner and suddenly stopped in a dome-shaped room. He couldn't believe his eyes. There the giant lay, its great chest heaving in deep sleep. Its hairy nostrils flared with every breath and wetness bubbled in the corner of its mouth. Bones, human bones, white and licked clean, were scattered all over the floor...

MONSTERS YOU NEVER HEARD OF

Raymond Van Over
With an Introduction by Colin Wilson

TEMPO BOOKS, NEW YORK

MONSTERS YOU NEVER HEARD OF

A Tempo Book / published by arrangement with
the author

PRINTING HISTORY
Tempo Original / October 1983
Second printing / October 1984

All rights reserved.
Copyright © 1983 by Raymond Van Over
Introduction copyright © 1983 by Colin Wilson
This book may not be reproduced in whole or in part,
by mimeograph or any other means, without permission.
For information address: The Berkley Publishing Group,
200 Madison Avenue, New York, N.Y. 10016.

ISBN: 0-441-53597-6

Tempo Books are published by The Berkley Publishing Group,
200 Madison Avenue, New York, New York 10016.
Tempo Books are registered in the United States Patent Office.
PRINTED IN THE UNITED STATES OF AMERICA

Contents

Introduction by Colin Wilson   vii

The Green-Haired Giant of China   1

The Demon Gebroo   13

The Monster of Croglin Grange   19

The Painted Skin   27

Black Magic   35

The Legend of the Beautiful Werewolf   41

The Golem   55

The Murdering Ghost of London   69

The Cannibal Giant Oo-mah   73

The Burr Woman   83

The Windigo   97

The Snake Woman of Wales   109

Nevillon's Toad   113

The Beast of Csejthe Castle   125

Acknowledgments   145

Introduction

by Colin Wilson

When the great Irish writer of horror stories, Sheridan Le Fanu, died in 1873, his face was set in a grimace of terror. For weeks before his death, he had been plagued by a nightmare of being in an ancient, tottering house, and he would wake up screaming that it was about to fall on him. When his doctor saw the expression on the face of the corpse, he commented: "I thought so—that house fell at last."

The horrors in Le Fanu's novels are peculiarly nasty because they have an air of genuine violence, like the police report of a murder case; you can almost hear the crunch of bone and spattering of brains. Even his ghosts are as unpleasant as slugs; a classic chapter in *The House by the Churchyard* describes a haunting by the ghostly hand—a plump, well-kept, rather aristocratic white hand, which scratches on windows and pushes its fingers through holes in the casement to try and undo the catch. When somebody lets it in, it begins scratching on bedroom doors, and then worms its way into the child's bedroom, and hovers above his head while he is asleep, giving him terrifying nightmares.

We can see here that Le Fanu was writing to *exorcise* his own deep fears. He is like a child who has heard that "something horrible" has happened to a neighbor, and urgently *needs* to know what happened, even if it makes him vomit, because anything is better than the unexorcised cloud of fear hovering like poison gas in a dark corner of the mind.

Raymond Van Over is an expert on world mythology, who has edited a number of volumes on the subject: sun myths, creation myths, hero myths, sacrifice myths, and so on. Like Jung, he recognizes that myths are an expression of the deepest longings and creative urges of the human spirit. But as I read this manuscript, I realized that he is aware of something that most of us have forgotten: that it is the myths and fairy tales of *fear* that symbolize the deepest problem of human existence.

It is, fortunately, easy for us to forget that feeling of vulnerability we had in childhood—the feeling that gives us a sense of helplessness, and somehow of uselessness, as if it negated all our feeling of value. I was haunted throughout my childhood by the image of a schoolboy who dived into a canal and sliced off his hand on a piece of rusty corrugated iron stuck in the bottom. But at least I could visualize what happened. When I read of Jack the Ripper disemboweling women, it was completely beyond my experience, and therefore produced that "grisly" feeling which is somehow worse than any horror we can visualize. As a teenager, I found in a second-hand bookshop a volume on medical jurisprudence, and opened it at a photograph of a man who had blown off his head by lighting a stick of dynamite in his mouth. I closed it hastily and pushed it back on the shelf. But outside the shop, this struck me as stupid. I went back in, bought the book, and took it back to my rented room, where I looked through it slowly, trying hard to control the lurches of my stomach at the sight of mangled corpses. But within an hour I was immune. Later, I used to enjoy showing the book to guests—particularly if they came to eat—to watch their attempts to control their nausea.

This is the basic adult reaction to that feeling of vulnerability—what Sartre calls "contingency," the sense of being a *victim*. We do not really outface the horrors; we merely grow an extra layer of skin over our sensitivity, so they cease to make us wince. But the result can be a form of self-deception. We see a headline about some unpleasant murder case, and think that we have learned to face up to the violence of the modern world. In fact, we have merely learned to look the other way.

This was a realization that struck me forcefully recently as I compiled an encyclopedia of modern murder. Detailing case after case of mass murder, involving mutilations or even torture, I recognized very clearly that murder has become far more unpleasant and far more cruel in the past twenty-five years since I compiled my original *Encyclopedia of Murder*. But what also struck me is that so many of the killers were curiously immature personalities—what psychiatrists call "autistic"—with no genuine sense of the reality of other people. Dean Corll, the Houston mass murderer, was photographed as an adult cuddling a teddy bear. Wayne Gacy, the Chicago homosexual killer, struck his neighbors as vulnerable and oversensitive, like a child. The German mass rape killer Joachim Kroll, who sliced chunks off his victims to cook and eat, was a mild little old man who thought the police would let him go home once they had castrated him and removed his insatiable sex urge.

What is obvious is that such people never faced up to that childhood feeling of vulnerability; they merely buried it under a pile of cushions, then remained obsessed by that dark cloud hovering in the corner of the mind. And this explains why I feel that this book of Rayond Van Over's is far more than a collection of gruesome fairy tales. What he has done is deceptively simple, and sheer literary skill has made it so easy to digest that the whole volume can be gulped down in one reading. Yet in this semi-mythological form, he has raised one of the most basic issues of our civilization.

The "fairy tale" produces in us a soothing sensation—the feeling we used to get as children when someone said, "Once upon a time..." For me, it brings back the delight of watching the curtain rise on a pantomime. Yet in these "fairy tales," we immediately find ourselves in the frightening world of Dean Corll and Joachim Kroll. Van Over has quite deliberately increased that element of nastiness, so that its flavor is not overwhelmed by the sheer interest of the story—as it is in tales like Jack and the Beanstalk or the Seven Wives of Bluebeard. As we read of Tobias's horrifying adventures with the Burr Woman, or Su Tung's encounter with the flesh-eating demon, or Pastor Grimm's creation of the Golem, we can re-enter the childhood world of terrors that waited on the other side of the front door on winter nights.

For me, they not only brought back that authentic feeling of childhood fear, but a flash of insight into the problem that has been troubling me as I compiled the *Encyclopedia of Modern Murder*. As I discovered my five-year-old self, still sitting there inside my fifty-year-old body, I experienced again his feeling that behind the security of home and parents there lay a world too frightening to be faced. The British poet laureate John Betjeman has a poem about a child returning from a birthday party, and the pleasant memories that "Hold me as I drift to dreamland/Safe inside my slumber-wear."

And I see that the world of Betjeman—whose poetry I enjoy as much as anyone—is essentially a warm, comfortable world of sunburned girls in tennis shorts and "little shuttered corner shops," a world in which you can feel "safe inside your slumber-wear." I also see that Betjeman has closed his books on the universe too soon. Unlike Ivan Karamazov, he feels no temptation to "give God back his entrance ticket," because he has turned his back on the darkness in the human soul. But at least, his world, like that of P.G. Wodehouse, is cheerfully and frankly one-sided. If I try to read the latest block-buster best-selling novel—one which apparently "tells the truth" about sex and cruelty and selfishness—I feel that it is equally oversimplified and one-sided, but that the author has become so skilled in self-deception that he—or she—will never realize it. The stupidity, the narrowness, the materialism of so much modern life and culture is again due to that essentially false reconciliation with childhood fears, the determination to hide them under a pile of cushions.

When Jung first realized around 1910 that he detested the narrowness of Freud's sexual theory, he began trying to create his own alternative in a book called *Symbols of Transformation of the Libido,* which was basically a long excursion into the mythology of ancient man. He was, in effect, pleading that we should open our mental windows and try to grasp some of the immensely exciting complexity of human history. It was more than half a century before his ideas began to percolate through to the reading public—and even then, in a diluted form that contradicted their essential spirit.

Now Raymond Van Over, another avid student of world mythology, has made an attempt to present the same plea with an almost childlike lucidity and simplicity. He defined his starting point in a letter to me: "All my life I have been fascinated by a few basic ideas: meaning, pattern structure—is there any? I've spent most of my life trying to find out the answer. The mind, the organizational stuff of consciousness. Individual realities and how the psyche creates and orders its perception of reality. This brings us to myths and how mankind uses art, the creative dynamic, to structure its own history. Without an inherent dynamic toward fulfillment, human life, it seems to me, would dissolve into the boundless...Myths help us structure and guide our destiny."

He goes on: "The subjects of these stories are, of course, horror. But with a difference. They are based on myths and legends that are not in themselves necessarily horrifying." And having spoken of frightening legends like "The Windigo," and "scary" or almost funny ones like "Nevillon's Toad," he gets down to the heart of the matter: "Still other stories represent powers of nature that defy our ability to cope. Ghost stories, werewolves, all things that 'go bump in the night' make us cringe because they are a fundamental mystery—not an academic problem, a mystery that logic can solve, but a mystery that transcends all the convenient systems we've created in order to function. These powers work according to other laws than those we are used to... Hence they terrify us. But even though they terrify us, they also allow us access into another world, into other dimensions. Myths and horror both open creaking doors into dimensions of life that show us other realities. If terror, fear, anxiety, is the price we must pay to open these ancient rusted portals, so be it."

These stories are, then, an attempt to awaken that basic terror that still comes to some of us in the middle of the night when we wake up and realize how little we know about this universe. A few rare human beings have genuinely outgrown these fears by outfacing them. The rest of us should be grateful for a reminder of a world that is more terrifying but also more replete with wonder and excitement than the "reality" we have come to accept.

The Green-Haired Giant of China

Night was coming and the chill air whipped through the forest. The shepherd had been walking all day, and for the first time since the attack he was frightened. He had fought off the hungry wolves. But all his small flock had been killed, except for the lamb he carried under his arm. He had barely escaped alive by climbing a tree with the lamb and waiting until the wolves had gorged themselves and carried off the carcasses of his sheep.

Su Tung was covered with bruises and his head ached, but he knew he had to keep going. He had nothing to eat, and not even matches for a fire. He couldn't survive another night in the forest unprotected, so he plunged on through the trees, hoping he'd find shelter before it got completely dark.

The night shadows moved swiftly, covering the floor of the forest like a crawling black fog, when Su Tung saw a flicker through the trees. He stumbled toward the light, which came from a fire sputtering before a run-down temple. An old priest was stirring something in a steaming kettle that hung over the fire. The sweet smell carried to Su Tung and his mouth watered. His stomach growled so loudly it sounded like thunder in his ears.

"Hello," he called to the old man. "I am lost and need shelter for the night."

The priest turned and looked at him for a long moment and then motioned him to the fire.

"Sit down, you are welcome at the temple of Kwan Yu."

He stirred the food and then poured some of the dark rice paste into two wooden bowls. "My name is Liu and I am the priest of Kwan Yu's temple."

"Why do you sit outside like this?" Su Tung asked as he drank the hot soup. "It is cold and will rain soon."

The old priest lowered his head and stared into the fire. "I do not enter the temple after sunset, and I have not done so in many years."

Su Tung, who was a bold young man, looked at the temple. There was indeed something about it that bothered him. Its cracked walls with roots and vines crawling over it, its dark interior that looked like a gaping mouth, were frightening.

All through the meal Su Tung was aware of the temple, as if something were inside waiting. As the night grew colder and the rain began to fall Su Tung turned to the old priest.

"Forgive me, Priest Liu, but I wish to take shelter

in the temple. I will leave my lamb beneath the verandah, if you don't mind."

The priest, who was himself shivering in the chill rain, stopped rubbing his hands over the fire.

"Young man, I wouldn't do that if I were you. I will be honest with you. The temple has been haunted by powerful and evil forces for years. Many have entered after dark and were never seen again."

The old priest huddled closer to the fire. "My task is not only to care for the temple, to repair it and give offerings on holy days to Kwan Yu, but to keep people from entering. Every time I have failed to keep strangers out of the temple, they have disappeared."

"What happened to them?" Su Tung asked.

"No one knows," answered Priest Liu.

"Well, I am not superstitious, or frightened of the unknown," Su Tung said. "Nothing could be as fearful as a pack of wolves. I survived that, so I am sure I can manage to spend one night in an old temple."

Su Tung took a burning stick from the fire to use as a torch and picked up his lamb. As he approached the temple steps Su Tung thought he saw a shadow move inside the doorway, a darker shape shift farther back into the black interior. It was a dark night, and his torch cast twisting shapes across the temple entrance. Su Tung smiled at his imagination. Tricks of the light, he said to himself.

The old priest stood up, his hood fell back from his head, and rain ran down his face.

"No," he cried out. "Please don't. I cannot stop you, but I am duty bound to warn you again. Don't be so rash, there are powers here beyond your understanding."

Su Tung turned to the old man. "Thank you, Priest Liu, for the warning. But I and my lamb are cold and wet, and I don't fear things I cannot see."

Su Tung raised his torch higher and peered into the black mouth of the temple. Again a dark shadow moved inside. Su Tung strained his eyes to see what it was. Nothing. All was still. Just the flickering shadows cast by his torch.

Su Tung mounted the steps and tied his lamb to one of the pillars when a sudden noise startled him. It was a swishing sound and reminded him of his mother mopping the floor. Su Tung hesitated and listened. Silence, only the sound of rain drumming on the porch roof.

He took a deep breath. He wasn't going to let a few night sounds or shadows cast by his torch frighten him.

He stepped into the temple holding his torch high and in front of him. He also clutched his shepherd's whip in his right hand. It was a short sheepshair whip that his grandfather had woven years before he was born. It wasn't much good for anything, but it was strong and made a loud crack when used properly and kept the sheep moving. Yesterday the whip had frightened the wolves enough to give him time to climb a tree. It had saved his life then and he felt better with it in his hand. He didn't believe the old priest's tales, but he wasn't going to take any chances.

With every step he took into the temple dark shapes seemed to shift, to move farther into the black depths. It was almost as if light frightened whatever it was—if, of course, there were anything really there.

Inside, the temple was much bigger than it appeared outside. The center room, which had a huge square altar in the middle, was so large the light from his small torch didn't reach any of the far walls. Even the door was now only a lighter shadow behind him.

Well, he thought, as he studied the altar, I might as well sleep here as anywhere. In fact, the heavy woven cloth covering the altar looked comfortable, so he climbed up, rolled his whip under his head for a pillow, and promptly went to sleep.

Su Tung had never been troubled by dreams, and as he had told the priest, he was a man who believed only what he could see and touch. But tonight his dreams were bad. Giant shapes draped in rusted chains formed out of the blackness and crept around him like huge slugs circling a waiting meal. The dream was so real he felt hot breath on his face as they hung over him, their squinting red eyes running hungrily over his body. They squealed in a high-pitched chattering, which even in his dream Su Tung thought odd considering how large and ferocious they were. It seemed they were hungry. The three largest creatures slapped and kicked at each other, but they mostly attacked the smaller, darker creatures that hissed around their flanks. The small black things backed off whenever the three larger chased them as they neared the altar. It was as if the three were saving Su Tung for themselves but for some reason could not quite reach him.

The dream so disturbed Su Tung, and seemed so real, that he tossed and turned on the altar. For one moment he almost fell off, and the hissing and spitting turned into a frenzy as all the creatures surged forward and grabbed for the leg that dangled over the altar's edge. Su Tung shifted his leg back onto the altar and the creatures again turned on each other with renewed fury. Su Tung had the uncomfortable feeling that being on the altar was the only thing that kept them from tearing him to pieces in their hunger. He was like a piece of meat hanging just out of reach.

Suddenly a loud scraping awakened him. He sat up in a sweat, terrified at the blackness. He peered wide-eyed into the dark, seeing nothing and hearing nothing. Then the heavy scraping noise again. It sounded like a large stone being moved. His torch was where he had left it, stuck into a crack in the corner of the altar. It was only a faint ember now. He brought it near and blew gently until the glow deepened and a small flame licked up at him. He kept fanning gently until once again it burned brightly.

He held it at arm's length and moved it in a circle around him. Nothing. Then he saw them. Three huge statues of the giants Kwan Yu, Liu Pei, and Chang Fei surrounded the altar. The center statue of the most terrible Kwan Yu was slowly turning. Its massive pedestal twisted in a widening circle and under its base the now trembling Su Tung saw a gaping hole. Wide stone steps led down into a blackness so dense that it seemed to twist and move before his eyes. From deep in the hole came a distant grunting, as if a herd of pigs were rooting under a rock. For the first time in his life he was too frightened to move. Su Tung held his breath and put his hand to his mouth to hold down the scream that welled up.

First a heavy hand larger than his head reached out of the hole. It was covered with thick hair and had long talons. Su Tung at first thought it the paw of a giant bear except for the long fingers that flicked in the air as if they were smelling the room. A massive head slowly emerged, its bulging yellow eyes glanced suspiciously around the room. It was a human face but unlike any Su Tung had ever seen, ugly and creased with a webbing of scars. Its eyes fastened on Su Tung and then it grinned; a row of fangs covered in green mold protruded beyond its fat lips. A long, thick tongue flicked out and swept wetly over its lips.

It lifted itself out of the pit and stood up. Su Tung was astonished. The creature was the height and weight of at least two men. It opened its arms wide and roared loudly, momentarily deafening Su Tung. Then it roared again and laughed and stamped its huge pawlike feet. Dust splashed up and filled the room, covering Su Tung and making him cough.

The giant abruptly stopped its dance and stared

at Su Tung. It lumbered forward grinning, as a hungry man comes to the dinner table. Even though terrified, Su Tung kept the torch steady and groped for the whip with his other hand. As the giant came closer Su Tung realized the long hair covering its body was green and curly, like moss crawling over a tree.

Su Tung snapped the whip forward; its tip cracked against the giant's chest and cut away a tuft of hair which arched through the air and floated to the floor. The giant stopped in its tracks. It had never been struck before. Never even resisted. All the others had panicked and wept, easy prey.

Then anger swept over the giant and it roared, its face twisted in a dreadful snarl. It lunged for Su Tung, who leapt aside at the last moment. The giant's knees hit the stone altar and it fell, sprawling on the floor and bellowing in rage. Su Tung was on his feet and running for the door. The air was heavy with lunging shadows and hissing, hesitant creatures. Black shapes flicked their tongues and plucked at him as he ran. But his panic was so great that he was like a stone hurtling through the air.

Then he was outside, panting with his face down in the mud, rain pelting him. The old priest walked over, his head sheltered from the rain by a small paper umbrella. He looked at Su Tung unbelievingly.

"Did you see it?" Su Tung gasped. "Did you see it? The giant. It was after me."

Su Tung sprang to his feet and pointed into the temple, his hand shaking uncontrollably. He grabbed the old priest's arm and started to pull him toward the forest. "Come, we've got to get out of here."

Liu released himself from Su Tung's clutching fingers.

"But there is nothing, my friend. Look, the temple is quiet."

Su Tung stared wide-eyed. Everything was silent, only the occasional restless shadow flitting back and forth.

"But... but, it was there. And many little hissing creatures crawling, that tried to get me," Su Tung stuttered.

"I heard and saw nothing until you ran out of the temple screaming," Liu said. "Come. Sit by the fire and get warm. I have some tea. It'll make you feel better."

Su Tung allowed himself to be led to the fire, which was sputtering under a lean-to Liu had constructed over it. They both huddled out of the rain, neither able to take his eyes from the temple door. Su Tung's teeth chattered. He seemed to expect something to come out of the temple at any moment.

Near dawn Su Tung finally spoke, once again his voice strong and determined. "I will not allow that *thing* in there to get the better of me. At first light I will go back in."

No matter how Liu tried to prevent him, Su Tung was determined. So when the sun rose and a shaft of light extended into the temple doorway, Su Tung rose and walked back up the steps.

He carried another, bigger torch, which he poked into the door first. Then he stuck his head around the corner of the entrance and peered in. With the morning light reflected into the temple he could see clearly. The great room was silent—and empty. The three massive statues stood mute in a half circle around the altar.

He stepped into the room, his whip ready. Nothing stirred. He touched the mighty statue of Kwan Yu. It was cold stone. Solid and unmoving. Su Tung pushed and the statue trembled slightly. He pushed harder and the stone gave way. The pit beneath slowly opened and Su Tung gazed down the steps. The pit stank something awful. It reminded him of when he fell into the pigpen.

Rotting meat and wet garbage.

Su Tung started down. The steps turned a sharp corner and suddenly stopped in a dome-shaped room. He couldn't believe his eyes. There the giant lay, its great chest heaving in deep sleep. Its hairy nostrils flared with every breath and wetness bubbled in the corner of its mouth. Bones, human bones, white and licked clean, were scattered all over the floor.

Su Tung considered. There was little he could do. If the giant awoke, he would be killed and eaten. He wasn't strong enough to kill it. In fact, there was nothing he could use, no weapon. He had been silly to come down here, it was useless.

Just then a fragment of burning wood from his torch fell on his hand and burned him. That was it. The answer. He ran quietly back up the steps and took all the dry wood from where Liu had stacked it under the porch roof.

His arms full, he carefully made his way back down the steps. Working hesitantly and silently he placed the wood around the giant. Several times the giant moaned loudly and shifted in its sleep, but soon Su Tung had finished. He took his whip and regretfully cut it in two. With one half he gently tied the giant's feet, with the other he laced its hands together and knotted the end to a metal ring on the wall.

He didn't know how long the whip would hold the giant, but it was strong and might be enough. Su Tung placed his torch to the wood and it immediately flared up. He ran to the stairs and watched. The giant didn't wake up, but began to twist and turn in its sleep. Then, as its long green fur caught fire, it screeched painfully and sat up. Its eyes wide and bulging, the giant stared at Su Tung, then at its bound hands. It tried to stand up, lost its balance, and immediately fell back into the burning pile of wood. The heat drove Su Tung farther up the steps and the stink of burning hair made him hold his nose. The huge body of the giant was now being cooked alive by the fire. It twisted and bounced, screaming horribly the whole time, but nothing could stop the flames.

It became so hot that Su Tung went up the steps and into the fresh air. Outside, he and Priest Liu listened to the screams for a long time. Finally there was silence and the smoke billowing out of the temple stopped.

Su Tung turned to Liu and bowed low. "I am sorry, Priest Liu, to have destroyed your temple and killed the spirit living in it."

Liu smiled at the young shepherd. "Don't be sorry," he said. "The temple is not destroyed. It still stands and will be like new after a good spring cleaning. As for the spirit you killed, that was not Kwan Yu but an evil creature that used the temple simply to feed upon easy prey. Kwan Yu's spirit thanks you, for it now may return to its home."

The Demon Gebroo

In a small African village called Gaffat there lived a powerful medicine man who was also the head of his clan. Chief Chibisa said little but was respected for his power over spirits and demons. But every so often a *Bouda,* or forceful animal demon, appeared and took possession of people. Every time Chief Chibisa tried to find and exorcise the demon, it somehow escaped.

One evening while Chief Chibisa rested at his home he heard a woman crying in the distance and many feet running. He peeked out the door and saw a woman on her hands and feet like a beast, grunting and waddling down the road. A small crowd followed her; some beat her with a stick while others hung back and watched.

Chibisa went out onto his porch as the woman approached. He clutched the bag of medicine that hung around his neck. The natives gathered around him and all began talking at once. "This is the Bouda," they said over and over. "If it is not driven out of her she will die like the others."

"Yes," one woman said. "Just like my brother."

"And my child," another voice complained.

"This Bouda had afflicted us for a long time," an old man said. "And we have never been able to kill it. Help us, please," he pleaded.

The old man looked at the woman groveling in the dusty road, rutting her nose and mouth in the dirt like a pig.

"This is my wife," he said. "I love her dearly. Can you do anything to help?"

As the old man said this the woman howled and raised her face to the sky. She kept howling as Chief Chibisa walked around her, wondering what he could do. He had once heard of a cure for possession by animals that was supposed to be effective. He decided to try it.

When he was ready he took hold of her head and dropped the juice of a white garlic into her nostril. She snorted and sneezed but immediately became docile.

"Who are you and why did you possess this woman?" Chief Chibisa asked in a strong voice.

"I was allowed to come into this woman," came the answer through her lips.

"What is your name?"

"Gebroo," it answered.

"And how many people have you possessed?" Chibisa asked.

"Forty people, both men and woman."

"You must now leave this woman's body before you are driven out and destroyed," commanded Chibisa.

The woman shook her head violently back and forth, snorting like a beast before she answered.

"All right. I will, but on one condition."

"What is it?" Chibisa asked.

The old woman smiled and licked her lips. Then the deep voice said, "I want to eat the flesh of a donkey."

Chief Chibisa laughed out loud. But when he saw the woman was reacting angrily he stopped and became serious.

"But why do you want this strange thing?" he asked. "Surely there is nothing special about donkey meat?"

"To me there is. It is a delicacy I rarely am allowed. If you give it to me now, I promise I will not only leave this woman but your village."

"And never return?" Chibisa asked.

"Never, I swear."

Chief Chibisa ordered the villagers to bring a donkey, which they did immediately. It was fastened by leather thongs to a stake. As soon as the possessed woman saw the animal she howled and sprang forward. She jumped on the donkey's back and bit into its neck, tearing off one piece of flesh after another.

The donkey kicked and bucked in panic but the woman clung to its back like a cat, her fingers digging into the animal's flanks. Her teeth gnawed and tore at the poor creature until it toppled over and died. The possessed woman crouched over it gnawing and licking until a large portion of the donkey's body was consumed.

At last filled, the woman looked up from the carcass. In her deep voice she said, "I am Gebroo. I have eaten and am pleased. I will keep my bargain."

The woman looked at the Chief and smiled. "But first I need one thing more."

"What's that?" answered Chief Chibisa.

"A child. A newborn child to take with me."

A wailing sprang up from the crowd, who had watched the grotesque feeding in horrified silence. "No, no, no," they cried in unison.

"That is too much," said Chief Chibisa. "I warned you and you have not kept your part of the bargain. You will not get a child."

Chief Chibisa took a vial from his robe and sprinkled its contents over the woman. Wherever a drop touched her the flesh sizzled and smoked. The woman screamed and tore at her burned skin, cursing and flailing about on the ground in agony. Chibisa continued to sprinkle the liquid on the woman until finally she flipped over on her back, her mouth gaped open, and a dense black smoke expelled from her. It came rushing as if there were no end to it, as if a fire deep inside the woman were being smothered and yet continued to burn. After a while the smoke became less dense and rose slowly out of her mouth, which now slackened. Her face slowly began to relax and then she suddenly fainted into a deep sleep.

When she awoke she was back to her old self. Her husband put his arms around her and led her home. The demon Gebroo was never heard of again.

The Monster of Croglin Grange

Croglin Grange is a lonely, small house near Cumberland in the northwest mountains of England. For centuries the house had belonged to one family, until in 1874 they decided to move south. The house was rented to an Australian, Edward Cranswell, who immediately moved in with his brother Michael and sister Amelia. The three young people were delighted with the place despite its remote location—until one humid summer night in 1875.

It was a beautiful night and the three stayed up till nearly midnight watching the silver light of the full moon stretch across the lawn. On the far side of the property was a ridge of trees, beyond which lay the ancient churchyard and cemetery.

When they separated for the night they went to their own rooms. But Amelia, feeling the heat was so great she couldn't sleep, opened the shutters and sat up in her bed, still fascinated by the beauty of the night. Slowly she became aware of two lights flickering in and out of the trees bordering the churchyard—low to the ground, like cat's eyes reflecting light. As she watched they emerged from the trees along with a dark shape, a definite ghastly *something* was approaching the house. Every once in a while it became lost for a moment behind a tree or bush, only to emerge again still coming closer across the lawn. As it came nearer and its shape became more distinct, an uncontrollable horror seized her. It wasn't her imagination, or her eyes playing tricks. It was a figure, a dark, misshapen form, jogging directly toward her window.

Amelia began to scream but found she couldn't. Her mouth was open but no sound came. Desperate to escape she jumped from bed and flew to the door, which was locked from the inside as her brothers always demanded. In her haste she fumbled the key and it fell to the floor. Blind with panic she scrambled on her hands and knees searching for it when she heard scratching at her window.

The window was next to the door and as she looked up a hideous dark face with glassy red eyes was staring at her. She screamed then, and the sound came as an enormous release. But the scratching continued, louder and more urgent now. And she screamed and screamed. There was nowhere to hide, nowhere to run, so she scurried across the floor to the bed.

The covers gave her a form of comfort, as did the knowledge that the window was locked. But the thing outside wouldn't be held back by either of these slim barriers for long. Suddenly the scratching sound stopped.

Silence. Nothing. Had it gone away?

Then a pecking sound. And scraping. What was it doing? Then she knew. It was unpicking the caulking around the glass. Faster and louder the sound came until suddenly a diamond-shaped pane of glass fell to the floor. A long bony hand came in and turned the handle of the window latch.

The window swung open and the creature came in. By now Amelia was trembling violently, her tongue glued to the roof of her mouth. She couldn't make a sound. The black angular thing came swiftly across the room and paused at her bed. Mute, she stared up into those hard, glowing eyes, unable to move.

A hissing sound then rushed from the creature's lips and it raised its gaunt arm. It grabbed Amelia's long hair and twisted it. Her head was yanked upward toward its face and then abruptly down again over the side of the bed. Almost in a trance now Amelia realized the creature was bending her head back, exposing her throat to it. Still grasping her hair tightly it twisted her head to the side and bit viciously into her throat.

Somewhere in the back of her mind, as if from a great distance, she heard fists pounding on her bedroom door.

Her brothers. At last. What took them so long? But it no longer mattered, she thought angrily. She was dead. It was too late.

When at last the brothers burst open the heavy

door they found Amelia unconscious on the floor. The thing had leaped through the window and Michael chased it across the lawn. He lost sight of it over the churchyard wall.

Edward stayed with Amelia while Michael took a horse and rode for the doctor. He did what he could for his sister, but she didn't regain consciousness.

The doctor arrived in a while and immediately washed her wounds.

"Merciful heaven," he exclaimed. "These are bites! What has gone on here?"

Edward and Michael stood passively watching. They said nothing. What could they say? They had no idea what sort of a creature it was. It looked like a man, but that was an insane thought.

Later, as they sat around the fire talking about it, the first theory the doctor came up with was that it was a dog. Edward and Michael had only imagined that the creature had the shape of a man. Amelia was equally hardheaded. When she regained consciousness and her composure returned she explained it away.

"What has happened seems inexplicable," she said. "But, of course, there *is* an explanation and we must simply wait for it. Perhaps a lunatic has escaped from some asylum and found his way here."

But then the stories came in from neighboring farms and nearby villages. Similar horrors had happened before. One little girl had been disfigured for life by just such a vicious attack. Several woman had screamed for help in time to escape permanent injury. Then the creature would vanish for a while. Only to begin again somewhere else.

This didn't shake Amelia's belief. Obviously the creature was an escaped lunatic, though there was no record of any.

The doctor, however, was worried about Amelia and when her wound healed he recommended to her brothers that they all go away for a short vacation. After some mild resistance Amelia agreed and the three traveled to Switzerland.

Amelia was a strong girl, so she threw herself into new activities in Switzerland. She climbed mountains, made sketches, and dried plants that she collected from the fertile valleys. But as autumn came it was she who became restless and suggested that they return to Croglin Grange. Her brothers were reluctant but Amelia insisted.

"We've rented it for seven years and haven't even been there one yet. We'd better return, and after all," she argued, "lunatics don't escape every day. Whatever it was has probably long disappeared."

But the brothers weren't so sure. Since the house was small Amelia had to remain in the same room. Edward and Michael insisted, however, that they stay together in a room just across the hall from their sister. And they also kept loaded pistols in the room. They were not taking any more chances and even insisted that Amelia always keep the shutters closed and locked.

The winter passed peacefully and happily. It was almost as if nothing had ever happened. Then one March night Amelia was suddenly awakened by a sound she remembered only too well—an intense scratching and pecking at her window. Without warning the wooden shutters cracked and the top slat was pulled loose. The same hideous dark and shriveled face peered in at her.

This time Amelia screamed as loud as she could. Immediately her brothers were out of their beds and, with pistols cocked, rushed into her room. Seeing she was unharmed they ran out the front door. The creature was already scurrying across the lawn. Michael fired and hit it in the leg but it continued to limp away almost without a pause. It scrambled over the wall into the churchyard and the brothers followed. It disappeared near a large vault that belonged to a family that had been extinct for years.

Edward and Michael searched the area but could find nothing. The vault's door was still locked and rusted.

The next day the brothers summoned all their neighbors and local officials to the churchyard. They explained about the attack and how they had traced it to the vault but then lost it. They demanded the officials open the vault to make sure the creature didn't have some secret entrance or hiding place there.

When the seal had been broken and the heavy rusted door forced open no one could believe their eyes. It was a bloodcurdling scene. The vault was full of coffins. Each one had been broken open and the corpses scattered over the floor. All were horribly mangled and distorted. Legs, arms, and heads were separated from the bodies. Some had been chewed to pieces, faces gnawed to the bone.

Only one coffin remained intact. The lid was loose, as if it had been moved, but still in place. Edward and Michael lifted the heavy wood. There it lay. Withered and brown, almost mummified, but quite complete. The same hideous figure they had seen running away from their home. There was the clear mark of a recent pistol shot in the leg.

Most of the villagers ran terrified from the place. But a few, along with Michael and Edward, lifted the creature from its box and took it outside where they promptly burned it.

Many believed later that it was a crazy, unnecessary violation of a corpse. A sacrilege of the church. But that was the last anyone ever heard of the creature from Croglin Grange.

The Painted Skin

One morning Wang was out walking when he saw a young girl carrying a heavy bundle and hurrying along by herself. Wang caught up to her and found that she was a very pretty girl of about sixteen. Suddenly shy and stuttering, he asked where she was going and why was she alone in the forest.

"I'm a traveler like you," replied the girl, who began to gently weep. "Don't bother yourself with me. There's nothing anybody can do."

Wang was very disturbed by her distress and asked her what was the matter. After a moment she told him her story.

"My parents were poor and they sold me as servant girl to a rich family. The woman of the house was very jealous and mean, and she beat me morning and night. It was more than I could stand, so I have run away."

The girl began weeping heavily now and Wang

tried to divert her by asking where she was going. She told him that she had no place to stay and was just walking.

"My house is nearby," Wang said. "Why not come there and visit? My mother is kind and would welcome you."

The girl smiled and immediately accepted. Wang picked up her bundle of belongings and led the way to his house. But on the way the girl made Wang promise to keep her presence a secret, for otherwise her life would be in danger. The master of the house she ran away from was looking for her and would kill her.

Wang promised not even to tell his mother or brother. The girl was impressed with Wang's home, for it was large and comfortable, and she chose to stay in a spare wing where no one would know of her presence.

Wang had agreed to the secrecy, but something about it disturbed him. Surely the master of a house would not follow a servant girl so far simply to kill her? It was hardly worth the trouble. Poverty existed throughout the country and finding servants was not difficult at all. Why would someone seek her out so passionately?

Several weeks passed and one day Wang was going into town when he met a Taoist priest, who stopped and stared at him as he went by. Irritated, Wang asked the priest, "What are you staring at? Have I put my clothes on backwards? Have my ears fallen off?"

The priest smiled briefly and then came right up

to Wang and sniffed him. All over. His face, his neck, his chest, even his hands and feet.

"What are you doing? Are you crazy?" Wang cried, jumping back.

But the priest wouldn't let go and clung to Wang's shirt, sniffing him intently. Finally he let go and looked deeply into Wang's eyes. "Why," said the priest, "you are bewitched. Who have you met recently?"

Startled, Wang blurted out, "No one. And besides, what business is it of yours?"

"No business of mine, sir," said the priest, smiling. "But if I were you I'd take this seriously."

"Well, you're not me. You're only a crazy priest. Now leave me alone," said Wang. He turned and walked away.

The priest shook his head as he watched Wang leave. "The fool!" he said. "Some people don't seem to know when death is at hand."

The encounter with the priest scared Wang. No matter how hard he tried, he couldn't put the old priest's words out of his mind. But then he couldn't believe a pretty young girl like his guest was a witch. It was probably just a priest wanting to do some extra business. A small charge for exorcising his home, Wang thought. Yes, that's probably what he was after. All these priests were money grubbers.

Wang returned from town later than he had planned. He decided to visit his pretty guest but found the door to that section of the house locked. This had never happened before and he became suspicious. He climbed over the wall and tried another door. It, too, was locked. Softly creeping to a window he peered in. The girl had her back to him and was busy with something spread out on the bed. As she turned the hair on his neck stiffened and his mouth dropped open.

The back half of her body was "normal," but the front half was inhuman. It was a hideous monster with a yellow-green face and jagged teeth like a saw. The skin glistened and rippled with scales. Heavy mucus hung from its mouth and eyes.

The creature turned back to its task. It dipped a brush into some paint and touched it to the human skin lying spread out on the bed. After a while it threw aside the brush and gave the skin a shakeout, just as you would a coat covered with snow. It flipped the skin over its head and pressed it down its body, running its hands smoothly from its face, down its chest and stomach, to its feet. After it had smoothed all the wrinkles it stood before the mirror and admired its beauty, smiling with the gentle, sweet turn of mouth that had so captured Wang.

Wang almost wept with fear, anger, and disappointment. He left the house and immediately sought out the priest. He searched for a long time until he finally found the old man in a cave. He threw himself on his knees, told the priest all he had seen, and begged him to help.

The priest answered Wang slowly. "You ask a great deal of me. I can hardly endure to hurt any living thing, so I do not wish to destroy her. The creature must be in great distress to be living in someone else's skin. For she could never accomplish this fraud without using real human flesh. I hesitate to think how she got the skin," the priest said sadly. "It must be a powerful demon."

Suddenly the priest stood up and faced Wang. "Here, take this fly brush and hang it at the door to her room. It will keep her imprisoned for a time until I can prepare something."

The two men agreed to meet later at a temple where the priest would give him a more permanent solution for getting rid of the creature.

Wang went home and hung the brush above the door. He could not bring himself to go in or greet the girl, knowing what lay beneath her beautiful skin. Just then he heard footsteps behind him. She was coming. Wang jumped behind a door and waited breathless. The girl came into the hallway and immediately saw the brush. She walked up to it and stared. Anger flickered across her face and she ground her teeth, but she turned and went back out the door.

Wang was relieved and returned to his room where he told his mother the whole story. She was shocked and terrified to have a demon in her house. Wang calmed her and told her to keep watch until the girl returned and then tell him everything that happened so he could relate it all to the priest.

In a short time Wang heard the girl return and go into her wing of the house. She was no longer quiet and spoke loudly with anger. Wang could clearly hear her cursing.

"Priest," she said fiercely, "you are a fool. You don't frighten me. Do you think I'm going to give up what is already in my grasp?"

She reached up and tore the brush down, pulling it apart and throwing it around the room. Then she spun on her heel and walked toward Wang's room. He could hear her heavy steps coming and cringed back on his bed. She burst open the door to his room and walked straight up to his bed, ripped open Wang's chest with a small, sharp knife and tore out his heart.

Wang's mother screamed and the servants ran up, crowding into the room. But the girl was already gone; only the miserable spectacle of Wang's torn body and the bloody room told the story of what had happened. Everyone was too terrified to pursue the girl, so the family spent the night weeping and cursing their ill fortune.

In the morning Wang's mother sent her other son to find the priest. When the old man found out what had happened he cried out in great rage, "Was it for this that I had compassion on you? Now I recognize you for the devil you truly are. There shall be no more pity."

The priest followed Wang's brother to the house, but no one knew where the girl had gone. She seemed to have disappeared from the face of the earth. But the angry priest was not easily put off. He raised his head and sniffed the air. Looking around, he circled the house sniffing, peering into crevices, blowing his nose and spitting on the ground. Finally he stopped and sniffed again, turning on his heel.

"Ah," he whispered. "There she is. She's not far off."

The priest turned to the brother. "Have any strangers come to the house today?"

Wang's mother spoke up. "Only an old woman looking for cleaning work. She is working in the house right now."

"That is she," the priest said. "Come."

The priest marched toward the house and stopped in the courtyard. "Come out, you miserable fiend," he yelled. "And give me back my brush. I have stronger medicine for you now."

The old man pulled a gleaming sword from his cloak and held it before him. The new cleaning maid came to the door. She and the priest stared at each other for a moment. Then the maid screamed and ran at the priest, who struck her down the middle. She fell flat, the human skin dropping off and leaving only a pulsing green muck that lay grunting like a pig, sucking air into its gasping mouth. The priest struck again with the sword and her head flew off. The teeth continued to chatter for several minutes but finally stopped and the head lay still.

The priest kicked the head aside and plucked at the loose skin, peeling it back away from the body. He carefully stretched it out on the ground. It was complete even down to the hairs of the eyebrows and eyelashes. As the horrified members of Wang's family watched, the old man gently rolled up the painted skin. He covered it with a silk cloth and turned to leave.

Wang's mother was weeping and crying out. She

threw herself in front of the priest and begged him to use his magic to bring back her dead son.

"My power is not equal to what you ask," the priest answered softly. "I'm sorry. But Wang was warned and foolishly went ahead without thinking of the consequences. Everything has a cost. I'm sorry Wang's was so high."

The old priest turned away with the painted skin under his arm and walked out of the courtyard and into the forest. He whistled as he went.

Black Magic

In his youth Mr. Yu was fond of boxing and other trials of strength. He was strong enough to lift heavy jars and throw them farther than anyone else in the village. He was proud of his healthy body but kind and compassionate to the weak. So when his servant became ill Mr. Yu went to a fortune-teller in the marketplace who was skilled at calculating the length of a man's life.

As soon as Mr. Yu entered the tent the fortune-teller asked, "Is it about your servant's health that you wish to consult me, sir?"

Astonished, Mr. Yu replied that he was right.

"The sick man will come to no harm," said the fortune-teller. "It is you, sir, who is in danger."

Mr. Yu was struck speechless. Then he asked the man to consult the oracles for him.

After performing his ritual the fortune-teller

looked horror-stricken. "In three days you will be dead," he told Mr. Yu. "But," the man continued, "I know certain magic arts and if you give me ten coins of silver I will avert this disaster for you."

To Yu's way of thinking, if his fate was determined no magic art could change it. Besides, he felt the fortune-teller was probably a fraud and just trying to make extra money with his sly prophecies of doom. So without saying a word Mr. Yu rose and began to leave.

"You deny a small charge," the fortune-teller said. "You'll be sorry for it. I can turn it against you as well as for you."

"You'll be sorry," he called again as Mr. Yu left the tent.

All his friends were concerned for him when they heard the story, for they were not as fearless as Mr. Yu. They advised Mr. Yu to go back to the fortune-teller and pay the fee. But Yu instead waited out the three days in his home. Nothing at all happened. When night fell on the third day he closed his door and sat alone in his room with a drawn sword at his side, for he didn't trust the fortune-teller.

The night wore on and nothing occurred. Yu was sleepy and about to go to bed when he heard a rustling outside his window. He turned up the light just as an ugly creature with boils and pits all over its head, bulging eyes, and fangs protruding from its mouth, burst through the window. Yu had never seen an ogre before but had heard them described looking just like this monster that fiercely leapt at him. He swung his sword with all his strength and felt it sink into the ogre's flesh.

The creature was cut cleanly in half. Mr. Yu watched in amazement as both halves of the body twitched and flopped on the floor. Fearing it may not be dead he hacked at it again and again, producing a dull thud each time, until it was nothing but small red pieces of meat scattered around the room.

The room was such a mess that Yu swept the remains of the creature out the door and cleaned the blood. Frightened now by the apparent power of the fortune-teller, Mr. Yu sat up for the rest of the night.

In a while he again heard scuffling noises outside. Peering out the window he saw the scattered pieces of the ogre wiggling along the ground, pulling apart and joining together, as if each piece was looking for its mate. Before his amazed eyes the groups of flesh grew larger and larger until they finally formed little mounds. The mounds then began vibrating and wiggling toward each other until they matched and built into larger pieces. Soon Yu saw a hand, a foot, an arm, a chest, a shoulder, and finally an enormous head. But this time the creature was huge, a giant ogre that struck Yu with terror.

The giant reached down and plunged his hand into the earth up to his wrist. With one mighty pull he yanked a shining curved sword out of the ground. The giant ogre opened his yellow jaws and bellowed so loudly that the doors and windows shook. Fearing that his house would be destroyed Yu went outside and immediately attacked the monster.

In the dim light from the moon Yu saw its coal-black face and glittering red eyes. The giant wheezed like an ox. It was covered with thick hair. The ogre roared again like thunder and threw a knife at Yu, who ducked at the last moment. The knife pierced the wall and quivered. Flushed with anger the ogre swung the sword over his head with a swishing sound and smashed it down on Yu. But Yu darted forward under the ogre's vicious downward stroke, which struck a rock and split it in two.

More enraged than ever the ogre swung the great sword again. Yu avoided the whistling weapon, but it cut off the lower part of his robe. Yu in turn hit out wildly, stabbing his sword up into the giant's armpit. The sword sank into the giant's chest and clanged like metal hitting hard wood. But Yu stabbed again and again as the giant stumbled backward. Finally the giant collapsed to its knees and Yu swung at its head as hard as he could. The head flew from the ogre's massive shoulders and fell to the ground. It rolled several feet until it crashed into a large rock.

Yu ran into the house and returned with a lamp. The ogre's body and head were part of a life-sized wooden figure with a sword strapped to its side. Where Yu's sword had struck its arms and chest, and all over the severed head, there was blood.

Yu sat up until dawn. He understood now that the fortune-teller had sent this monster to kill him and thereby prove his magic powers. As soon as it was light Yu went to the magician's tent and found him cowering in a corner. Yu held a knife to his throat and called the police, who came and arrested the magician. He was later tried and found guilty and put to death.

The Legend of the Beautiful Werewolf

The forest suddenly became silent, as it always did when something was about to die. The beast slid like a shadow through the moonlight and stopped behind a tree. Its blood-red eyes watched the man. It was not a large animal but it twitched with violent energy. It clicked its long talons and snapped its paws open and shut.

The man seemed to grow nervous as he came closer, sensing something was wrong. Suddenly and without warning the beast plunged through the brush. The man turned, panic on his face, and raised his hands to protect himself. But the wolflike creature hurtled itself through the air and knocked him onto his back.

"Get off, get off!" he screamed, fighting frantically to keep the beast away. Its wet muzzle pressed under his chin. He could feel the heat of its foul breath. It smelled like something dead, he thought, just before the creature sank its fangs into his throat. The beast lifted its head toward the full moon and gave a long, wailing howl.

It was about this time that a hunter was returning home, his bag full of rabbit and quail. When the unearthly sound had filled the forest he stopped, his senses alert. He had never heard an animal cry like that and it sent a chill up his spine. The howl had been close. Too close. He cocked his gun. And waited. Nothing but silence and his own breathing. Not a sound throughout the forest. It was as if everything were waiting. Then a soft grunting came from just ahead. He moved forward cautiously. The sudden stillness of the forest and the guttural grunting terrified him. He was an expert hunter and had killed many dangerous animals, but for some reason he was more frightened now than he had ever been before.

As he approached the curve in the path the terrible cry came again and the hair on his neck stiffened. He wasn't sure he wanted to see what lay ahead.

When he turned the corner the beast looked up, its piercing red eyes nailing him to the spot. It snarled. At first it looked like an exceptionally large wolf, but its eyes and ferocity were somehow demonic and the hunter felt its power like a wave of heat when opening a stove door.

The beast was angry. It started toward the man stiff-legged, hackles high on its back. Its eyes never wavered from the man. The killing lust had risen again like a sudden fever.

The hunter knew that unless he acted he only had

a few seconds more to live. But he was unable to move. His knees trembled and almost collapsed under him. He forced himself to stay on his feet and face the beast. It was his only chance.

Suddenly the beast charged when it was still far down the path. The violence of its attack shocked the hunter into action. He yanked his rifle up and pulled the trigger just as it leaped at him. The shot hit its leg with such force that the beast flipped over in midair. Still, its charge was so fierce that its hurtling body knocked the hunter to the ground.

The hunter lay stunned on his back. His first thought was, I am a dead man. His rifle had been flung from his hand and he was defenseless. The beast was only wounded and he'd be quickly torn apart. He braced himself for the attack, but instead there was a painful howl and the beast disappeared almost immediately into the forest, leaving a thin trail of blood behind.

After a moment the hunter picked himself up, made a sign of the cross, and thanked God he was still alive. That creature was a demon straight from a nightmare. He could still smell its breath, stale and laden with decay. The beast's paw lay on the ground nearby. He examined it closely. It was unlike any he had ever seen. It was shaped like a wolf's paw, but the talons were exceptionally long and sharp, similar to a large cat's.

The hunter stuffed the paw in his game bag and started after the trail of blood. It led him to a village deep in the forest that was surrounded by a high wall. A magnificent castle towered above the village. The trail disappeared at the wall. There was no blood anywhere on the stone, and no hole the creature could have gone through. The hunter went to the village gate and rang the bell.

In a moment a small window in the huge wooden gate slid open and a voice said, "Go away. The village is closed for the night."

Surprised, the hunter replied, "I've wounded a dangerous animal and the track led here. Let me in so I can find it."

A long silence followed, then the voice said, "Go away. It is the master's order that the gates be locked at sunset. No one may enter after that, especially on a night of the full moon."

The small window slammed shut. The hunter rang the bell again and again until the window snapped open. An angry face filled it. "Don't you understand? I cannot open the gate. Only the Count can give permission after the sun sets."

"Well, go get it, then," the hunter yelled back. "Or I'll stand here and make such a racket all night that no one will sleep a wink."

The window slammed shut again and the hunter waited. In a while the great wooden door creaked and slowly swung open. A sullen gatekeeper peered out, looked anxiously around, and motioned the hunter to come in.

"Hurry, hurry, you fool. Don't you know how dangerous this is?"

As soon as the hunter was inside the gatekeeper slammed the wooden bar into place.

"Follow me," he said and turned into the narrow,

winding streets. Soon they arrived at another heavy door. The gatekeeper took a large key from a ring that hung at his side and inserted it into the lock.

It was then the hunter saw the blood splattered on the wall. The gatekeeper started through the door and up the steep stairs that were cut into a solid rock tunnel.

"Come on," he said irritably. "The Count doesn't like to be kept waiting."

The hunter said nothing about the blood but kept his rifle cocked and ready. The creature could be anywhere. As they climbed the dark tunnel a distant moan echoed down the stairs. It was a cry full of pain and anger. Both the hunter and gatekeeper stopped abruptly. The flickering light from the lantern cast grotesque shadows on the walls. The eerie wail from the darkness above them, the damp, musty smell of the tunnel and the wet, slimy stone were too much for the gatekeeper. He broke into a cold sweat. And when another, even louder moan wafted down the shadowed stairwell he turned to flee. The hunter grabbed him by the shoulders.

"Wait," he hissed. "It's not near. That's just the echo making it sound so close."

"What is it?" the gatekeeper whispered.

"I think it's the beast I shot."

"But . . . but what is it doing here? In the master's castle?"

"Haven't you heard it before?" the hunter asked. He felt sure he knew the answer now. This was its lair. The beast was some sort of demonic creature that preyed on humans. Probably a werewolf.

The gatekeeper stuttered, "There are always strange sounds in these old buildings. Sometimes it's like the wind, other times wolves crying in the forest. But nothing like this."

He trembled and shook like a dog with wet fur.

"It sounds like an angry child, doesn't it?" the hunter said. "But still, it's not quite human."

The hunter pushed the gatekeeper up the stairs.

"Come on, let's go. It doesn't help to stand here."

Several more times the inhuman wail rang down the stairwell as they climbed ever higher. The hunter pressed on, urging the gatekeeper to have courage. Finally they came to another door. It, too, was smeared with blood but the gatekeeper again didn't seem to notice.

The door opened into a great hall of the castle that led to the Count's private quarters. The gatekeeper warned the hunter to be careful with the master. He was a man with a quick temper and his wrath was often terrible. He ruled the village with an iron hand.

The Count didn't bother to rise when they entered his study, but the hunter could see he was a big man. His face was flushed from drinking and heavily lined.

"Well, what do you want?" he asked before they were introduced. "It had better be important to get me out of bed," he warned.

He scowled and drank deeply from a tankard of hot wine.

The hunter answered boldly, "Deep in the forest tonight I wounded an animal and followed it here."

"So," the Count growled. "What does that have to do with me?"

"The beast is wild and very dangerous. I came upon it just after it killed a man. If it has a lair here, everyone in your village is in grave danger."

"Nonsense." The Count laughed. "We have our own hunters and don't need any more."

"Your hunters won't help you against this creature. Unless they know something about the black arts and killing werewolves."

The Count's face went suddenly chalk-white. His hand shook as he took another drink.

"I don't believe that superstitious nonsense. Werewolves, vampires, ghosts. That's for ignorant peasants."

"You're wrong," the hunter said. "I've seen things that are not of this world. And I tell you this beast is part devil. Its paws are like a wolf's, but with the talons of a cat."

"Here, look at this." The hunter reached into his game bag, but instead of the paw he had shot off he pulled out a human hand.

Stunned, the hunter stared at the pale, stiff hand. So, the creature was a werewolf. What other animal could alter itself like this—even after death? He was surprised to still be alive. He had not been prepared for hunting werewolves and had no protection against the supernatural powers. No blessed ammunition, or bullets bathed in holy water. No silver bullets shaped for the werewolf's heart.

The hunter studied the frail hand. His shot had severed it at the wrist in a jagged bloody line. A large obsidian ring glinted brightly on the middle finger. He touched it and yanked his hand back. It was hot as fire. His fingertips were burned white.

Just then the Count jumped from his chair and grabbed the bloody hand. He turned it over and over, then let out a groan and closed his eyes tightly as if he were in great pain.

Seeing his expression the hunter asked, "What is it? What's the matter?"

"The ring," he moaned. "The ring. It's my wife's. I gave it to her myself."

"See," he said, pulling it off the stiff white finger. "I had it inscribed."

The hunter read the delicate writing inside the ring. "To my beautiful B."

In a choked voice the Count said, "When we were married Beatrice swore she'd never take it off."

The hunter was confused. He didn't know what to say. It was hard to believe this was the Countess's hand, for he had never heard of a female werewolf.

Softly the hunter said, "Perhaps there's some mistake and we should talk to the Countess?"

The Count stared at him as if he didn't understand the simple words. "Yes," he replied coldly after a moment. "Perhaps we should." He turned and walked from the room with the hunter hurrying to catch up.

Without knocking the Count burst into his wife's bedroom. The curtains were drawn around a large four-poster bed, and the hunter could barely make out the shadowy figure inside. A peculiar smell filled the room. Then he recognized it. Mold. Damp, musky mold. The kind that grew on dead trees during the rainy season. His quick eyes noticed the blood on the windowsill. Another red smear was on the wall near the bed.

So it was true, he thought. A woman can be a werewolf. What a fool he'd been. He hoped that she had already turned back into her human form. If not, and she was still a werewolf, they were both dead men. He lifted his rifle and made ready even though he knew it was useless. He couldn't inflict a mortal wound on a werewolf. Wound them, yes. But never kill them with normal bullets.

The two men approached the curtained bed but were stopped dead in their tracks by a low, throaty snarl. It was a growl straight from hell and made the hunter's hair stand on end. Neither man moved. The bed shifted and the curtains waved slightly. The hunter could make out the dark form behind the gauze. It shifted from side to side, moved toward them, and then backed off.

It's undecided, thought the hunter. But why? Because of its pain? Because it's home, in its human nest, and not used to killing here? Sweat trickled down his back and his hands trembled as he leveled the gun at the thing behind the curtain.

What to do? If he shot he could not kill it. But it would attack soon and it could kill them both in seconds. He searched the room desperately. There was nothing he could do. No escape. He had seen the creature's incredible speed and realized he would never make it to the door. Then he saw it. A long, thin silver letter opener on the Countess's writing desk. It was not blessed by a holy man, but it was silver and might be enough. It was better than lead bullets.

Slowly, ever so slowly, he inched sideways toward the writing desk. It seemed to take forever. The thing in the bed alternated between a guttural animal snarl and a whimpering human cry.

When he reached the desk he carefully put down his rifle and clutched the silver letter opener in his sweaty hand. He had made up his mind to attack. It would give him the advantage of surprise. It wasn't much, but it was better than doing nothing. He slowly moved toward the bed. He glanced at the Count, who had stood like a statue all this time, staring at the curtained bed.

The hunter said a silent prayer, took a deep breath, and lunged for the dark figure in the bed. For one silly moment he couldn't find the opening and tore wildly at the curtain. Then it exploded outward, tearing loose from the bed frame and cascading over him like a collapsing tent. He threw off the curtain and stared in disbelief. The creature clung to the Count, its arms wrapped around his neck, the rear legs tearing at his belly. It looked like a weird dance as the two struggled to stay upright, their arms locked around each other's neck.

The creature was half-human and half-beast. Its body was still partially covered with heavy black fur. The legs and head appeared to be purely beast, although the paws had already begun to change to hands and feet, the talons now long, human fingernails. This made its furious tearing at the Count's belly futile, otherwise he would have been torn open immediately. The muzzle of its wolf face was still there, as were the sharp fangs.

The hunter jumped to help the Count, who kept thrusting the beast away from his face. Even now, while still only half-beast, the creature's ferocity and power were terrible to behold. The hunter grabbed the beast from behind, locking his arm around its throat. It swung its head back and forth trying to bite his arm. He had dropped the silver letter opener in the struggle and could do nothing now except hold on for dear life.

The two men managed to keep the creature between them until suddenly it hesitated, gasped loudly, and went limp. They cautiously released their hold and it fell to the floor. As they watched, the beast slowly dissolved and in its place lay a beautiful woman. The dark hair on its face was the last part of the beast to go, turning into a light down on the woman's fair skin.

The hunter was awed by her rare beauty, marred only by the blood scattered over her body and the stump where her hand had once been. She had tied a ribbon around it to stem the bleeding but it still seeped slowly from the wrist.

The Count's face, shoulders, and hands had been badly cut and servants rushed to care for his wounds. He was pitiless with the Countess. His first words were to order her chained in the castle's dungeon. Then she would be burned at the stake.

The Countess regained consciousness as the servants were chaining her to the prison wall. She begged for mercy but the Count simply glared at her silently. Finally he said coldly, "I have no pity for any of my animals that displease me. For years you have deceived me, hunting at night like a wild animal, and you will be treated just the same as a beast gone bad."

From that moment the Countess did not speak another word. And the next morning she was brought to the village square. Her wrist had been bandaged and the Count had allowed her a clean gown in which to die. The Count and the hunter watched silently as the wood was piled high and she was tied to the stake. She didn't utter a word, but never took her eyes from the Count's hard face.

When the fire was lit she became restless and strained at her bonds. The hunter at first thought his eyes were playing tricks on him as the smoke and heat rose in waves to cover her. Then he was sure. She was again changing into the beast. Her mouth widened and fangs forced her beautiful mouth open into a painful groan.

The flames licked higher and she snarled at the crowd like a wounded dog. She raised her head and said something to the Count. The hunter couldn't understand it over the noise of the fire and the excited murmurings of the crowd. Then she shrieked so loudly he understood.

"You've abandoned me, but I shall not die," she screamed at the Count, whose face had turned ghostly white. "I will return. I am in your blood. I already possess you."

The Count turned away and walked quickly from the square. He disappeared up the narrow stairs to the castle.

The hunter could watch no more. The Countess's face and hair were engulfed by the flames and her screams had stopped. Only a dark, smoldering figure hanging limply at the stake remained—a shadow amidst the dancing flames. The hunter did not want to wait and watch the Count slowly turn into a werewolf. For the Countess had been right, she was already alive in his blood. The hunter knew that once bitten by a werewolf the victim turns into the half-beast, half-human killer of the full moon. But the hunter was tired and didn't want to see any more.

The Golem

Pastor Grimm was a lazy man and his greatest joy was to sit in front of a fire doing nothing. There were only two things that disturbed his peace, the Sunday service he had to give to the few members of his church, and the daily chores around his small farm on the outskirts of the village. But as lazy as Pastor Grimm was, he was also a master of magic and had become expert in casting spells. One cold evening as the sun set he cursed his misfortune at owning his few animals for he didn't want to go out and milk his cow or heat the barn. He was comfortable in front of his fire reading his book of magic spells, so he decided the cow could manage one night without being milked. After a while he fell asleep and when he awoke it was morning. The fire had gone out and he was chilled to the bone. Shivering, he remembered he had not taken care of his animals so he rushed outside to the barn. There he found the dead cow and two dead chickens. They were all frozen stiff.

He cursed and pulled his ear, which he did whenever he got angry. No milk or eggs again for a while. This was the last time something like this was going to happen. What good were all his spells, all his knowledge of magic, if he never used them to make life a little more comfortable for himself. Right then and there he decided to do something about it. For hours he poured over his old books. Finally he decided to make a servant. Someone who could do all his chores and allow him the freedom to study. He would make a Golem. There were dangers, but he would be careful. He would need help, for he was an old man and not too strong. There was much physical labor involved, so he sent word for his nephew Jakob to come to him that very evening.

Jakob was not a very smart young man, but he was good natured, loyal, and very impressed with the learning and wisdom of his uncle Grimm. He would do anything his uncle asked of him and be proud to help.

Pastor Grimm told Jakob very little of what he planned. But he swore Jakob to secrecy and told him not to be afraid, no matter what he saw. Pastor Grimm packed a bag with all his magical needs, his large book of spells, and he took Jakob to a desolate part of the woods near the Vlatava River. Under the ghostly light of the full moon he had Jakob trudge back and forth between the muddy banks of the Vlatava and a small clearing where he had drawn a large circle. Then he had Jakob pile the muddy clay high in the center of the circle until he could no longer reach the top. Pastor Grimm sat down before the dark mass of clay and studied it. He measured it with his eyes, sketched the shape he wanted and then pulled out his large, leather book and leafed through the pages until he found the right spell. He repeated it over and over in his mind, pronouncing every syllable until he was sure he knew the spell by heart.

Pastor Grimm then had Jakob help him shape the rough form of a man. There was so much clay that when they were finished the figure was huge, at least seven feet long and as wide as two men. Pastor Grimm told Jakob to stand aside, and say nothing about what would happen next even on the pain of death. Jakob promised and Pastor Grimm walked to the figure's head, whispered a few words, and began to circle around it to the right. All the time he walked he whispered ten words, which he had told Jakob were combinations of the Divine Names. When the words were properly combined they attracted energy necessary to create a living being from lifeless matter. *Alef*, he murmured, *Beis, Gimmel, Dalet, Hay, Vov, Zayin, Ches, Tes, Yud*. He circled the figure seven times and then he stopped at the head and again repeated the ten words.

Jakob waited breathlessly. Nothing happened. Pastor Grimm looked up at Jakob, who was terrified that he would ask him to do something, anything. He was a simple man. He knew he would make a mess of it, whatever it was.

Then the figure trembled and began vibrating

gently. Jakob stared, too terrified to move. After a moment it let out a harsh sucking sound, followed by an agonizing moan. The chest heaved and its clay-dark face twisted into a peculiar grin.

Jakob couldn't take his eyes from the monster sucking in its first breaths and whispered, "Is it possible? Is it really happening?"

Pastor Grimm was satisfied with his work and looked over at Jakob and smiled. "Of course it is. The magicians of ancient Egypt took dust from under their feet and made creatures who did whatever they wished." He opened his book again and read: "First the human form sucks up warm air. This is transformed into water, then into blood. And from the blood is made flesh. When the flesh becomes firm, man is made."

Jakob stared at the dark clay. He couldn't see any flesh yet. But the body was now shaking violently, its arms and legs jerking as if it were being electrocuted. The hands grasped like a drowning man as its fingers dug into the hard earth. Jakob moved farther back into the woods, the hair on his neck stiff with fear.

Pastor Grimm walked around the figure again mumbling an incantation. When he finished his circling he stopped at the head and took a piece of paper from his pocket. He placed the folded paper in the figure's gaping mouth and said loudly, "When the miraculous Shemhamphoras is said over it, life spills in. *Emeth.*"

Suddenly the figure bolted upright and sat on the ground looking straight ahead. Slowly it turned its head, the face expressionless. No surprise, no wonder, Jakob thought. It accepted. It waited for instructions.

Pastor Grimm smiled and said, "Come, follow me." The monster clumsily got to its feet and stumbled after Pastor Grimm, who had already started to walk home. After a moment Jakob got the courage to follow, but he kept a safe distance back.

"You are a Golem," Pastor Grimm said to the creature. "You were born to obey me. You must do anything I say without hesitation, even if I ask you to walk through fire or jump off a cliff."

When they reached home Pastor Grimm took the Golem upstairs to the attic, where a small room had been prepared. The Golem would work during the day, sleep in the attic at night. Pastor Grimm would tell anyone that saw the Golem that it was a mute who had wandered by looking for work.

Before Jakob left Pastor Grimm came up to him and said, "You must never speak of what you have seen. There are dangers. Once alive the Golem cannot speak and understands things only dimly. But it has great, inhuman strength. It can uproot trees, lift large boulders, even shake a house to ruin."

Jakob swore he would never say anything and then ran all the way home. He knew he could never be in the presence of the Golem without trembling.

Emil the Butcher sweated a lot, especially when he was nervous. This night he was sweating heavily, for he was finally going to get his revenge on his enemy, the miserable and lazy Pastor Grimm. He had a wonderful plan that would ruin the Pastor.

He got excited just thinking about getting back at the man who humiliated him in front of the town council, who ridiculed his idea of stuffing food down the throats of caged geese in order to fatten them faster for the market. He and the other butchers would have made a fortune if the farmers had been convinced. A partnership or guild between butchers and farmers, once in a lifetime a man gets an idea like that. And it was all ruined by Pastor Grimm.

Emil put a heavy woolen scarf around his neck, stuffed his thick fingers into gloves, and went out into the cold evening. The sun was just setting so he had to hurry. He walked quickly to the playground, circled around to the woods behind, and stood in the shadows watching the children.

He didn't have long to wait for it was getting dark quickly now; the shadows in the forest were already blacker and longer. The children were hurrying, calling out good-byes, grabbing their schoolbags, books, and toys, and rushing off in different directions. Like little ants, Emil thought. It wouldn't be long. Since it was late some of them would have to take the short-cut through the woods. A group of three, one girl and two boys, came toward him. He stepped back into the shadows and waited, his hot, hurried breath turning white as he exhaled.

Emil followed at a safe distance until one of the boys split off from the others with a wave. Sweating under his heavy coat even in the near-freezing air, he picked his way through the now dark woods carefully. He made little noise yet the boy began to glance nervously over his shoulder. Emil felt he had to act quickly, they were getting too close to the road. Moving faster, he closed the distance, pleased with his agility.

The boy must have heard or sensed something for just as Emil was on him he turned, his eyes wide in panic, and lurched forward in a run. Emil puffed after him, cursing, but the boy was screaming in fright now and thrashing through the woods like a wounded deer. The boy was getting away. In anger and frustration Emil grabbed a large broken branch about the size of a fire log and hurled it. It hit the boy in the legs and he tumbled forward, crying out in pain. Emil was on him at once, his knife out of his pocket. He killed the child quickly.

Emil then unwrapped a sack from his belt and stuffed the body into the bag. Emil was still sweating, but not as heavily, as he swung the sack over his shoulder and started back through the woods. He whistled softly as he walked. Everything was going perfectly.

Two hours before dawn Jakob's wife shook him awake. He had his chores to do. Grumbling, he put on his clothes and went to care for his animals. When he was finished he came back in, had his breakfast, and then went out to harness the horse. Soon he was on his way to town with his milk, cheese, and eggs for sale. As he approached his uncle Grimm's house he saw a man with a sack over his shoulder standing behind some trees. Jakob was immediately suspicious and stopped a block away from the house, then ran back and knocked on Pastor Grimm's front door.

Pastor Grimm's anger at being awakened passed quickly when Jakob told him what he had seen. The old man went immediately to get the Golem. To their surprise it was already standing, facing the door. A sudden fear climbed Pastor Grimm's spine. The Golem had been waiting. But how could that be? He can't do anything without my orders, Pastor Grimm thought.

The Golem stood silently watching them. Pastor Grimm found his voice and said loudly to the Golem, "Go outside and find out what the man with the sack is doing. If he's making mischief, stop him."

Emil was just about ready to start for the barn when a horse and wagon startled him. He waited for it to pass and then crept into Pastor Grimm's barn. He opened the sack and placed the child's body under some hay. He smiled. The rest of his plan was simple. A brief note to the police about where to look and then he would start the rumors about Pastor Grimm's black magic. The body would be part of Pastor Grimm's evil rituals. And that would be the end of him. Emil grinned broadly at the thought.

A sudden movement in the shadows caused Emil to look up. A giant figure stood watching him. Emil screamed as the monster leaped at him. The butcher was a powerful man and he struck back, but it did him no good, a moment later he was dead.

The Golem dragged the limp, fat body to where the child was partially covered with straw. The monster stopped and looked at the dead butcher, then at the child. Now that everything was quiet, it was puzzled, and didn't know what to do. It turned and started back toward Pastor Grimm's house.

Pastor Grimm didn't bother to question the Golem about what had happened but went to see for himself. He found both bodies and shuddered. What had he created? Had the Golem killed both of them? Why was the child's body cut in two? For the first time in the months since he had created the Golem, Pastor Grimm began to regret his action. It was such a stupid creature and often made a mess out of the simplest tasks. Like the time he told it to bring water from the stream to fill the rain barrel. He had failed to tell it to stop once the barrel was full. When he returned home the house was flooded and the Golem was still pouring water into the overflowing barrel. But this, two dead bodies.

Pastor Grimm went back into the house and slowly and carefully told the Golem to get the bodies in the barn, leave them deep in the woods, miles away from home, and return before dawn. The Golem did as it was told and carried the bodies, one under each arm, several miles through the woods. As the Golem crossed a small field a farmer and his two sons saw the huge man carrying the bodies. They yelled for the giant to stop but it kept on walking, without even turning its head. The three men ran after the Golem and jumped on its back. They pummeled its legs and arms and tried to make it loosen its grip, but the Golem barely paused and continued to walk until the farmer and his sons dropped to the ground from sheer exhaustion.

The Golem walked on into the woods for another mile or so, then stopped, dropped both bodies and turned back. Later that day the bodies were discovered by a search party led by the farmer and his sons. Rumors about the monster spread quickly, terrifying the village. When Pastor Grimm heard what had happened he was more angry at the Golem than he had ever been. He was very tempted to destroy the Golem right then and there. But then he remembered how the Golem could work nonstop, how spotless the house always was, and how all the chores were done so quickly. He decided to give it another chance, for he dearly loved the times he sat in front of his fire reading his books.

For several months after the killings Pastor Grimm kept the Golem hidden. It only went out at night to do the chores and cleaned the house during the day. It swept and cleaned, carried the firewood, and beat the dirty rugs. And then it happened. The first time he wasn't sure if the Golem had understood him. He had told the Golem to go to his attic and lie down. He was reading a book at the time and something made him look up. The Golem was still standing there, staring at him. A chill ran over his flesh.

"Why are you here?" he asked. "I told you to go to bed." The Golem simply stared back, its large eyes unmoving.

"Golem," Pastor Grimm commanded forcefully, "go to bed."

The Golem slowly and, it seemed to Pastor Grimm, resentfully started upstairs to his attic. Pastor Grimm was sure the Golem was resisting orders.

Time proved him right, for the Golem began to take small actions on its own. It now often took longer to obey him. And one night he even found the Golem staring in his bedroom window when it should have been in its attic. These were all small things, but to Pastor Grimm they were telltale signs that the Golem was developing a willpower of its own. The thought terrified him.

As more days passed Pastor Grimm noticed that the Golem seemed to be growing. It seemed heavier and slightly taller. By the next week he was sure and he became even more frightened. The Golem had grown so large and so willful that Pastor Grimm began to fear for his life. What if the Golem became angry? Nothing on earth could stop it. He could only tell the monster what to do, but what would happen if it didn't obey?

Pastor Grimm pondered the problem and finally decided that the Golem must die. The monster had been useful, but it was too dangerous now. The old man went to his books and found the rituals he needed. First he had to get the magic word *emeth*, truth, out of its mouth. By erasing one letter he turned the word into *meth*, which meant "it is dead." He then had to put the death paper back into its mouth and the Golem would die.

He went upstairs to the attic. The Golem was sitting silently on a wooden chair near the small window. It seemed even larger than yesterday. Was it growing so fast? Pastor Grimm shivered, fear tingling over his skin. If he failed to kill it, would it continue to grow forever? Would its willpower become complete?

The Golem didn't move but Pastor Grimm felt its eyes on him. Did it sense he planned to kill it? He ordered the Golem to open its mouth. Slowly the monster's jaws opened. The paper lay crumpled on its tongue just as he had placed it. He put his fingers in and took out the paper. The Golem's eyes followed his every move. He took the paper to the table and sat down. The single candle flickered as he whispered the magic words of life in reverse, "Yud, Tes, Ches, Zayin, Vov, Hay, Dalet, Gimmel, Beis, Alef." He carefully erased the letter "e" and breathed a sigh of relief. It was almost over. He stood up and turned and gasped. The Golem was standing close behind him. Pastor Grimm was again amazed at its size. He was sure it had grown, for it towered over him like a dark tree. But what frightened him the most was that it had moved by itself, for some reason of its own. What kind of thoughts went on behind those blank eyes? He trembled, suddenly cold. Why had it moved? What would it do next? He swallowed hard and clutched the magic paper of death in his hand.

"Golem," he said in a stern voice, "open your mouth again."

The Golem looked at Pastor Grimm for a moment

and then slowly its dry lips parted. The small man tried to put the death paper on the Golem's tongue but couldn't reach that high. It had grown too big. He stretched on his tiptoes but still couldn't do it.

Pastor Grimm thought for a moment, then ordered the Golem to bend forward, which it did. His hand now just barely reached the dark mouth and he quickly stuffed the death paper into it. The Golem shuddered, its eyes staring down at Pastor Grimm. Suddenly a gust of hot, foul-smelling breath exhaled from the Golem's open mouth. Its face stiffened and Pastor Grimm watched, fascinated, as the Golem slowly turned to a dark, hulking statue of clay.

It was now dead and Pastor Grimm was relieved. But it was still terrifying. So huge and threatening, it leaned like a twisted column of stone above him.

A loud crack filled the room. Pastor Grimm looked around but could see nothing. Then there was another loud cracking sound like breaking bones. Suddenly he saw it. The hard clay of the Golem's body was cracking into hundreds of small lines. He looked up, the face was covered with spidery lines that made the lips seem to smile in an awful grimace. The huge figure tottered and began to fall forward.

Pastor Grimm realized what was happening too late. He tried to get out of the way but there was no time. The Golem's massive towering form fell forward right on top of him. The heavy clay crushed Pastor Grimm flat and then crumbled into dust over him. After a moment the attic was still again. The candle flickered over the mound of earth covering the small man. It looked surprisingly like a grave.

The Murdering Ghost of London

Some years ago Lady Madelaine Denis was traveling through London and stopped at an inn on the outskirts of the city. Only one room was available on the main floor at the back of the hotel. The window had iron bars and looked out onto a wide alley that ran along the back of the house. The alley was quiet and damp but clean, and Lady Denis decided it would be all right for only one night. She was very tired after two nights in a train and went to bed early. She was asleep almost immediately.

Sometime late in the night she was suddenly awakened by a loud noise of scuffling feet and a choking, gurgling sound, as if someone were struggling to get his breath. She lay very still, every nerve tingling and every muscle tense, and listened intently. The noise came from the window, which was shut. The dark alleyway outside suddenly seemed full of danger and her heart beat quickly.

She reasoned that with the window locked, and the heavy bars, no one could get in. Yet she still felt a cold dread.

What were those terrible guttural gasps that came in from the darkened window? Was someone being murdered? The frenzied struggle that became louder could only mean violent death. She lay shuddering as her imagination visualized the scene in the alley. But then the sounds shifted and seemed almost to be coming from inside the room.

If someone was being murdered it was clearly her duty to run to the window and cry for help, but she was paralyzed with fear and pulled the covers tighter around her neck. Though the window on the alley was well lit from outside, the blinds were drawn and little light came into the room. And she had only to reach out her hand to switch on the light next to her bed, but the paralysis of fear held her tightly.

Then the noise became so loud Lady Denis could not stand it. It was a dying agony, with convulsive, ghastly groaning and the thud of pounding and wrestling bodies. And even though her fears kept tugging at her she threw the covers back and leaped out of bed. Blind fury with her cowardice overwhelmed her paralysis for a moment and she ran toward the faint light at the window and thrust aside the blinds. But the alley was empty. There was nothing. And the street was so well lit that she could see everything clearly.

Lady Denis stood there silently, quivering with

excitement, not knowing what to do next. The sudden stillness unnerved her further. Then a sensation of raw terror took possession of her once more. An unreasoning sureness of her own death clutched her heart with an icy grip, for the noise began again, but now it came from behind her. In her room.

She turned toward the sound, two dark shadows straining against each other. The tallest man stood over the other, who was on his knees. He was squeezing his victim's throat in powerful hands and soon the man stopped struggling. Only a gurgling sigh came from him as he died. The tall man let the body drop to the floor with a dull thud. He was panting with exertion.

The killer turned to Lady Denis, who stood transfixed, and stared into her eyes. Trembling, she stepped back and pressed against the wall. When the tall killer stepped toward her she crumpled to the floor, unconscious.

When she awoke the sun was up. She looked toward the body but there was nothing. The room was empty. Peaceful and innocent, filled with the light of a cheerful summer morning. Her relief that there was no body was immediately replaced with the realization, with the absolute certainty, that a murder had indeed taken place in this room. And she had been a witness to its ghostly re-enactment.

Lady Denis packed her bags and left the room as quickly as she physically could. But she couldn't resist the temptation to ask the innkeeper whether "unfortunate" things ever happened in the inn. After at first denying anything unpleasant had ever occurred, the innkeeper admitted that there had been a murder many years before. In fact, someone had been strangled in her very room.

The Cannibal Giant Oo-mah

The Kwakiutl, a tribe of Indians who lived in the isolated high mountains of North America, were in constant fear of hairy giants they called "Oo-mah," or the "Big-foot." The giants did not often show themselves, but now and then hunters were attacked by them, or children who wandered too far from the camp mysteriously disappeared.

One night after the attacks started again, Chief Wakini called his family to him and warned them about the giants. He was worried because two of his sons, Elder Brother and Sun Boy, had come of age and were going into the forest alone to hunt mountain goats.

"They do not bother the white man," he explained to his sons, "because they don't like his smell. But they are always very hungry and like to eat our Indian flesh, so we must be very careful."

The old Chief stirred the ashes in the fire and

looked at his sons with concern. "My own brother was taken when we were children."

"Watch," he said seriously, "for brightly colored smoke in the mountains. That is the Oo-mah's campfire and they are cooking human meat. Stay far from that place, for the Oo-mah can smell human flesh for miles."

The next morning Chief Wakini walked with his sons to the edge of the forest and warned them again.

"Be careful, my sons. The Oo-mah are brutal and very dangerous. Listen for their whistling. That is how they talk between themselves. It is a high sound, like a hawk screeching but more musical. Some say it is beautiful, but few who have heard it ever return to speak of it."

He wished he could protect them from the fierce Oo-mah, but he knew his sons had to begin living their own lives. Their fate was falling like water from his hands into their own. He blessed them as they disappeared into the trees.

The two boys walked all day high into the mountains where goats lived. As the afternoon sun was setting and the mountain shadows deepened in the valleys Sun Boy grabbed his older brother's arm.

"Look," he whispered. He pointed across the base of the mountain to a nearby valley where a bright-colored smoke rose high into the sky.

"That must be a camp of the cannibal giants," said Elder Brother.

After a moment Sun Boy grinned and looked at his big brother. "I would like to see these creatures.

I can't believe they are more terrible than the grizzly bear that chased us last summer."

"I don't know," said Elder Brother. "Remember Father's warning."

"We will be careful. Let's just sneak up and watch. We are good hunters and even frightened deer can't hear us until we're close enough to spit at them."

Sun Boy's excitement won over Elder Brother, who also smiled. And away they went down the valley toward the ominous column of strange smoke.

On the way down Sun Boy tripped and cut his leg. It was not bad but the wound bled heavily. Elder Brother put a bandage around his brother's leg and suggested they go back. But Sun Boy was determined. It was only a slight wound, he said with a laugh, and he wanted to at least *see* a giant before they left. So they continued down the valley, moving cautiously now because they were close to the smoke, which they could see rising through the trees ahead.

On hands and knees they crept up to the entrance of a large cave hidden at the base of a cliff. It was from here the smoke poured out and streamed into the sky. They watched the cave door but could see nothing. No movement. No sound.

Sun Boy began to get restless. "It is getting late," he said. "Let's move closer and see if anyone is home."

The two brothers moved silently through the brush until they were almost at the entrance. It was so dark inside they couldn't even see the fire that caused the smoke to billow out above their heads.

"The cave must be very large," said Elder Brother. "There aren't even any shadows from the fire on the cave walls."

"Perhaps no one is home," whispered Sun Boy. "I'm going to go in."

"No," Elder Brother said urgently, but Sun Boy was already at the cave entrance. Elder Brother shook his head. He had to take care of his younger brother, so there was nothing he could do now except follow.

Once inside they were blind. It was so dark that their eyes could make out nothing, not even different shades of shadow. Soon their eyes adjusted and they could see a faint glow farther into the cave. They crept toward it slowly, their eyes and ears alert.

The cave ballooned out into a vast, dome-shaped room. In the center was a fire burning brightly. It momentarily blinded them after the dark tunnel, and they couldn't see into the shadows flickering on the cave-room walls. Then out of the gloom a movement startled them. Sitting along the far wall was an enormous hairy woman holding a giant baby in her arms. The woman and child were both staring at them with bulging, unmoving eyes. The brothers didn't move a muscle as they watched the giant woman suspiciously.

But the hairy creatures didn't move. Instead she whistled softly to her baby, who looked up at her and then over at Sun Boy. The young Indian suddenly realized they were looking at his leg. The giant baby, whose fat, soft body was also covered in hair, began to drool uncontrollably and whistled excitedly to his mother.

"He looks like a fat caterpillar," Sun Boy murmured to his brother.

"Yes," whispered Elder Brother, tightening his grip on his hunting knife. "But I think he eats more than leaves. Be careful and don't move until I say so."

Elder Brother looked at the giant woman and said bravely, "We are hunters of the Kwakiutl and have come to pay our respects to you and your family."

The woman's ugly face, which had a huge, bony brow and puffed, broad lips, smiled briefly.

"Scrape the blood off your leg for my baby," she growled in a voice that sounded like a bowstring on the bark of a tree.

Sun Boy looked at his brother, who nodded his head. He picked up a stick and scraped the blood from his leg, walked carefully over to the woman, and extended it toward her. Her hand flashed out and grasped the stick. She brought it close to her nose and sniffed, then smiled at the brothers and handed the stick to her baby. The child seized it hungrily and stared at Sun Boy as he licked it clean.

When he finished the baby began gnawing the stick. In a moment he threw it down in disgust and looked up at his mother and whistled urgently. She immediately hummed back with a gentle cooing, but without taking her deep-set, bulging eyes from Sun Boy and Elder Brother.

The baby's happy slurping scared them, but it was the mother's unwavering cold stare that unnerved them most. Elder Brother slowly lifted his bow and arrows from his shoulder and held them at his side. Sun Boy saw this and followed his brother's lead.

Elder Brother stepped back one step and said slowly, "Well, we must go now. It is late and our family expects us home."

When both brothers backed farther away the giantess suddenly spoke in her rasping voice. "No. You will not leave. You will stay for supper."

She then threw her head back and laughed. The sound sent chills down their spines.

Elder Brother snapped an arrow into his bow and let it fly right at the hairy mother's head. In a split second, too fast for the human eye to follow, the giantess shook her head violently and caught the arrow in her teeth, cracking it in two. The pieces fell from her mouth as she grinned at the boys.

"Stay, young things. My baby likes you. He wants to play, don't you, sweet?" she crooned to the child. The little monster gurgled and spit. The mother licked his face clean with her long tongue.

"See," she said to the boys between licks. "You get him all excited. Stay and play."

She set the child down. "See. He likes you. There now," she said, patting the little monster on his bottom. "Go play with the delicious boys."

The child tottered toward them, barely able to stay upright. Even as an infant this creature was taller and heavier than they were. The two boys kept backing away as the giant child clumsily followed them, grinning and drooling.

Smiling, the mother watched her baby, when abruptly she lifted her head and cocked it to one side. Listening. Suddenly she whistled, a high, intense burst. Both Sun Boy and Elder Brother heard the response, distant but clear. It was coming from outside the cave.

"It must be the father returning," Elder Brother said, his voice trembling. "There is no escape. He's outside the cave entrance."

The giantess continued to "talk" in her high-pitched whistles, occasionally stopping to listen.

"Probably telling him supper's ready," said Sun Boy sarcastically.

The giant baby fell with a *whump* and began rumbling toward them on his hands and knees. He was much faster this way and jumped excitedly from side to side, giggling and whistling gently at them. They could almost understand the baby's strange crooning. "Come to me. Come play with me," it seemed to be saying.

Sun Boy and Elder Brother had reached the tunnel that led back to the cave entrance. But the giant baby was now only twenty or thirty yards away. He could cover that distance in three or four easy leaps.

"Now," said Elder Brother. "Run for your life."

They turned and dashed into the tunnel and ran nose-high into the hairy pillars of giant legs.

Flat on their backs they stared up at the monster. He was ugly beyond belief and stood at least the height of two normal men. His arms and taloned hands were so long they reached easily to his knees.

Sun Boy and Elder Brother scrambled to their feet and backed away, their mouths open in amazement and fear.

"Wheeeee..." came the high, gurgling whistle from behind them. They spun around. The child had risen to his feet again and with arms outraised wobbled toward his father.

"Shoot the baby," whispered Elder Brother urgently. Sun Boy looked at his brother uncomprehendingly.

"But why?" he began. "We can't escape."

"Do it," urged Elder Brother. "Kill it."

It made no sense, Sun Boy thought, but he trusted his brother so he grabbed an arrow, notched it in his bow, and launched it into the baby's head. He let out a sickening cry and clutched his eye, dancing wildly in a spinning circle until he fell groaning to the ground holding his head.

As the shocked father watched his baby lurch in its grotesque death dance, Elder Brother strung an arrow and shot it into his throat. As the giant Oo-mah fell to his knees, Elder Brother and Sun Boy dashed around him. They could hear the giantess screeching, a part beast howling and part Oo-mah whistling.

Even as they sprinted out of the cave entrance they felt the earth trembling. The thunderous pounding was rhythmic. Giant footfalls running. Over their shoulder they could see the mother Oo-mah dreadful in her ferocious anger, chasing after them.

The two brothers ran as never before. They flew through the forest, whizzing past trees, leaping fallen logs, bursting through thickets and branches. But the Oo-mah kept following, slowly gaining on them, her giant strides easily catching up and surpassing their more rapid, smaller steps.

All during the wild chase the giantess kept up her unearthly whistling screech. Both brothers were tiring, their leg muscles burning with the effort, lungs gasping for more air. And still she gained on them.

Sun Boy, who was faster than his older brother, called back over his shoulder, "If we can make it to the river gorge..."

"Yes," gasped his brother. "Run, don't...talk."

The gorge was only another half mile. It was a sharp precipice that fell steeply to the river a hundred feet below. Both brothers knew their only chance was to throw themselves over and let the swift currents of the river carry them to safety. If they survived the fall.

Sun Boy was well ahead of his brother, who was now stumbling with exhaustion. Suddenly Elder Brother fell with a groan and tumbled over and over. He lay panting on the ground as the giantess caught up with him.

Sun Boy glanced behind him and shuddered to a stop. "Brother!" he cried, and began to run back.

"No!" Elder Brother yelled. "Go on.... Go!"

That was all the time he had. Sun Boy saw the giantess deliberately smash her heavy foot down on his brother's head. She glanced with satisfaction at Elder Brother's body as she started toward Sun Boy.

Groaning with misery, Sun Boy turned toward

the river gorge. He sobbed as he ran, weeping for his lost brother. The giantess was close behind him now. She would be on him in moments, but he could already see the edge of the gorge ahead. He heard her panting whistle behind him as he launched himself into the air.

As he fell toward the water he cried out in pain, "Bro...ther...For...give meeeee...."

The Oo-mah stood on the ledge and watched Sun Boy plunge into the river. She moaned and whistled softly to herself. She could not swim. But she would be patient and watch. She knew his smell and would search all the world if she had to, until she found him.

The Burr Woman

Tobias Smollet was a small man, but he was a dynamo. He had come to the little community in New Mexico only a few years before from the East and had already built the run-down ranch into a busy cattle and poultry business. The only trouble was that Tobias was as mean as a snake and twice as quick to strike.

The ten or so men who worked the ranch for him took it stoically. They listened, shook their heads, chewed their tobacco, and ignored him. The only reason they all hadn't been fired was that they did their job well and no one else would work for him. But, though no one could stand Tobias, he met his end in such a nasty fashion that even those who hated him the most were sorry about it.

The day it began Tom Longman, the fourteen-year-old orphan who'd wandered in off the desert one day, was riding back from town with a full wagon of supplies. Tom knew Tobias took him shopping so one of the men wouldn't be taken off more important work on the ranch, but he didn't mind. It was fun to get to town every couple of weeks. What he couldn't stand was the constant criticism. The old man just wouldn't leave him alone. Sometimes Tom thought he kept him on just to have an easy target to browbeat. All the other hands kept clear of him, but Tom couldn't, he was around the house all day long doing chores.

The day was hot and the red sand road dusty, just like every other trip to town. And just like every other trip Tobias had criticized how Tom loaded the wagon.

"Now, look at that," Tobias said as they bounced along. "The load has shifted."

Tom glanced over his shoulder. True, it moved a bit. But so what, the road's rough. Everything's going to move.

"Stop! Didn't you hear me?" Tobias shouted. "The load's shifted. It's going to fall off."

Tom looked again. Nothing was going to fall. Just another of Tobias's fits. Oh, well, Tom thought. I'll do what the others told me. Cater to him and keep my mouth shut.

Tom reined in the horses and pulled on the wagon brake. He jumped down and started to shift the load around. It wasn't necessary, but he made it look important. Tobias watched, his lips puckered together.

"Come on, come on," Tobias said. He jumped down from the wagon and walked over to a tree near the road and stood in the shade. He fanned himself with his Sears Roebuck catalog as Tom tried to tighten up an already secure load.

Tom did as much as he could and turned to call Tobias when he saw it. A small black thing flitted quickly between the tall cacti. There it went again. It moved like a blink of the eye. If you weren't looking right at it you'd miss it. Tom saw it again, this time only about twenty yards in the desert beyond where Tobias was standing. It seemed to be moving closer to Tobias but Tom couldn't be sure. He wasn't even sure it was anything alive. It might've been a dust devil. Or a blowing tumbleweed that looked darker than normal.

Then it came clear. It moved across a ten-yard clearing to reach another cactus and Tom saw what looked like a big monkey. It ran like one of those chimps, upright but still using its front hands so it sort of loped. But it wasn't a monkey. It couldn't have been. It was wearing clothes. Or rags. Long, dark rags that floated behind like a small, tattered cape as it ran.

"Mr. Smollet," Tom called, now alarmed. For he was sure the thing was making for Tobias.

Tobias turned toward Tom just as the thing leaped out from behind a nearby cactus and launched itself through the air. It was amazing to see, Tom later told the other men. The leap must have been at least ten feet. And it landed squarely on his back.

Tobias's face opened in shock. His eyes and mouth almost popped out of his head as he let out a loud "oouff" and hit the ground face first.

Tom ran to him. He was clawing the dirt and groaning in terrible pain. His face was still pressed into the dust. The thing on his back was just about the size of a large monkey, or a very small human being. But Tom couldn't see any real shape to it. Where there should have been a head there was only long, gray, scraggly hair hanging every which way. Something like hairy, pale hands were dug into Tobias's shoulders but Tom couldn't be sure if they were human or not. What might have been filthy feet were curled around Tobias's waist, the long toes clinging as if they were fingers. The thing had grabbed him so tightly you couldn't see where it began and Tobias left off. It looked just like he'd magically developed a hunched back. Hesitantly Tom reached out and touched the thing. A tremble ran through it, like a horse's skin shaking off flies. But Tobias went crazy. He screamed and rolled over onto his back. Then again and again, rolling in the desert, trying to dislodge the thing. But the more he rolled the tighter it seemed to grab him. And that made Tobias cry out even more.

Tobias jumped up and ran around in a circle, fell down on his back, rolled over, and then jumped up again. All the time screaming in pain. Tom tried to catch him but Tobias was like a madman, crying and yelling. Tears streamed down his face. Then he began backing into the tree, banging the thing as hard as he could. Time and again, he'd run forward five or six feet and then backpedal with his short legs pumping like pistons until he smacked into the tree.

But every time he'd do it Tom could see the pain shoot across his face. Tom admired his courage, because he didn't stop until he just fell from exhaustion. He didn't move for a long time and Tom thought he must have fainted. But the thing moved. It shifted a little and seemed to snuffle down even closer. If that was possible.

When Tobias woke up his panic was under control, but Tom could see he was still terrified.

"Take me home, Tom," was all he said, and climbed into the wagon.

When they reached the ranch Tobias sent for Doc Friday. While everyone waited for the doctor to arrive Tobias locked himself in his office and all the ranch hands gathered around Tom and peppered him with questions about what happened.

When Tom finished the story no one said a word. Then Saul, the cowboy whose face was covered with pockmarks, broke the silence.

"The Burr Woman," he said quietly.

Everyone looked at him. Raoul, the stocky Mexican, said, "Ah, *sí*. We have her in Mexico, too."

"What the hell is a Burr Woman?" someone asked.

"She's an old hag the Indians fear. There are legends that say once she gets on someone's back nothing can get her off. No one knows where she comes from or anything about her. Except the Indians think she's very powerful medicine."

"Bull," Randy Oakes cut in loudly. "That's superstitious junk."

"Yeah, well what would you call that thing on Smollet's back?" Saul asked, irritated.

"I don't know, but it sure ain't some Indian tall tale," Oakes said, getting up and pulling on his belt.

This was a sure sign of a fight coming on and Saul sat back and smiled. He loved to get Oakes mad.

"Listen, Randy. I'm not saying it's a Burr Woman. But I've heard about this before and it's the only thing I can see that fits. If something's beyond your little brains, why not just shut up?"

"I think you've shot off your mouth for the last time," Oakes said, starting around the table.

Just then Doc Friday came in and everyone started talking at once. Once more Tom told his story. When he finished Doc went into Smollet's office without a word.

After about five minutes Tobias let out a howl that shook the windows. The office door flew open and Doc put his head out.

"A couple of you men get in here."

No one moved.

"Now!" Doc yelled.

Saul and Tom were closest and Doc grabbed their arms and shoved them in the office and slammed the door.

Tobias was sitting on a stool, his shirt half-torn off his body.

"Come here," Doc ordered. "One of you on each side. Now, grab her wrists here," he said to both men, pointing. "And pull when I say so."

Saul and Tom searched for a way to get their fingers under the bony, emaciated wrist that seemed glued to Tobias's back. There was just no space where the Burr Woman's body pressed against Tobias's. Tom got his fingers partly under the wrist and squeezed as hard as he could. He guessed Saul did the same thing.

Doc got behind the Burr Woman and grabbed her on both sides. He braced his feet against Tobias's chair and said, "Pull."

Everyone tugged at once and Tobias wailed in pain. Tom felt the Burr Woman's body tremble and jerk itself down closer against Tobias. The harder they pulled the tighter her hold on Tobias seemed to get. After several minutes of yanking on her they all stopped, exhausted.

Tobias slumped over in his chair and sobbed. Doc pulled out his pipe with trembling hands.

"Well, I guess that's it," he said. "I've never seen anything like this in all my days."

"Here, look at this." He motioned for Tom and Saul to come closer. Doc gently pressed around her fingers.

"When you're gentle she doesn't fight back so violently. But she still lets you pull her away only so far.

"See," he said, pointing to where her fingers dug into Tobias's flesh. "It's almost as if her fingers have grown into Tobias's skin."

Doc gently moved back her gray hair and Tom saw a wrinkled, narrow face and one unblinking eye glaring defiantly up at them.

"And here," he said, pointing to where you could see her thumb angle back toward the spine. "Her thumbs dig right into the skin on each side of the spine. Look. If I just tug a little."

Her response was immediate and strong. The thumb pulled against the pressure and dug deeper into Tobias's back. Tobias jerked and cried out.

"It must be incredibly painful. Every time she's pulled away she digs deeper."

Doc straightened up and looked sadly at him. "I'm sorry, Tobias. There's nothing I can do. I doubt that her grip would loosen even if we killed her."

Tobias looked up hopefully at the thought.

"Kill her. Sure, why not? And then cut off everything except the fingers. I don't care if they're left in. Just get her off me."

"But look here, Tobias. Even her toenails are dug in. You want to walk around the rest of your life with two hands in your neck and back, and two feet stuck into your flanks?

"Yeah," Tobias pleaded. "Anything. Just get her off."

"I can't kill her," Doc said. "I don't know how much of an animal she's become. But from what I see she's at least part human. And I can't kill someone part human."

"Part human. My God, man. Nothing human could do this. It's a beast. Get the damn thing off me. I'll pay you anything. Anything. You name it."

"Tobias," Doc said softly, "to be frank, I'm not sure that you would survive our killing her."

Tobias's shocked face turned to Doc.

"It's almost as if she's become a part of you," Doc continued. "I just don't know how *much* a part is all. If it's as I suspect, you may die along with her."

"Oh, my God," Tobias moaned. "I can't live my life like this. I might as well die right now. Kill me and get it over with."

His head fell forward and he began to sob. Doc went to his bag and gave Tobias a shot.

"This'll keep him quiet. Put him to bed. There's nothing else I can do."

Doc walked out of the room shaking his head and mumbling to himself. "Oddest thing I've ever seen."

In the weeks that followed everyone seemed to accept Tobias's strange condition. It was as if he'd come down with an incurable illness and there was nothing anyone could do about it. All the men, however, kept their distance from him. Even though no one believed she'd jump from Tobias onto anyone else, they weren't taking any chances.

Tom still did the house chores, so he saw more of Tobias than anyone. Whenever Tom was near Tobias he couldn't keep his eyes from the hump. The Burr Woman never moved, only adjusted herself occasionally with that peculiar shiver of hers. Tom noticed that when she did tremble or shift slightly Tobias didn't seem to mind anymore. In fact, he'd adjusted to her presence with surprising speed. It seemed they were becoming a single person.

But Tobias was looking worse with every day. He was pale and often complained about terrible fatigue. Tom also noticed the Burr Woman was talking to Tobias. He couldn't hear much of it because she whispered mostly when they were alone. The few words he did hear scared him. One day he heard her raspy voice murmuring, "Dear, I'm thirsty." Another time, "Sweetheart, let's go for a walk."

At these moments Tobias sometimes shook his head violently and talked back. And an urgent, rapid, whispered conversation would take place. Eventually, Tom noticed, Tobias would do what she wanted. It was as if Tobias were struggling to keep possession of his body, or as if his brains were slowly being sucked into the Burr Woman. Every time Tobias resisted too vigorously Tom could see pain flash across his face.

About a month after Tobias had been jumped by the Burr Woman, Tom took his breakfast in. Tobias was lying on his side, as he usually did now, with his eyes wide open.

"Come here," he whispered so softly that Tom could barely hear him. "And be quiet."

Tom hesitantly walked over to the bed.

"She's asleep," Tobias said quietly. "Early in the mornings like this I'm free. If I move even a muscle or speak too loudly, she'll wake up."

"Listen," he said urgently, his voice full of anxiety. "Help me. I can't live like this. Kill me. Please, I beg you. Get my gun from the table over there and kill me. Do it. Now."

His eyes pleaded with Tom, his face twitching with the effort to remain quiet.

"Please, Tom. Before she wakes and begins to

take over again. I won't last much longer anyway. She's sucking me dry. My life's being sucked from me every day through these tentacles she's got in me. Shoot me. Please, please. Kill me," he moaned.

Suddenly Tobias's face twisted in pain and he groaned aloud. His body stiffened, his arms and legs springing into rigid poles. He began trembling and moaning, and sweat poured off him. Then his feet swung over the edge of the bed and he sat up, back straight, and stared ahead blankly.

Tom saw it happen. He slipped from being himself into a thing, into a movable statue. And the Burr Woman was pulling the strings.

Tobias's head swung toward the breakfast tray and he said softly, as if to himself, "Eat."

It was a hollow voice, echoing out of Tobias's mouth from a great distance. He got up slowly and sat down in front of the tray and began to eat slowly, mechanically.

For several days nothing else unusual happened. Then one morning Tom noticed Tobias was suffering more than normal. Every step seemed an agony. His pale face was constantly bathed in sweat. Every time his eyes met Tom's there was a question, a pleading. Tom knew what he was asking, but he couldn't kill someone. He'd never hurt anything in his life and the thought of killing Tobias made him sick to the stomach.

That day Tobias and Tom went to check the cattle water holes. The trail led along a ledge that fell straight into a forty-foot-deep gulley. Tobias had gone to sleep as the wagon slowly made its way along the rutted path. His white, exhausted face had fallen forward on his chest.

For some reason, an instinct perhaps, Tom glanced over at Tobias and saw that he was awake. He hadn't moved from his slumped position, but his eyes were wide open and darting about wildly. His head didn't move but he was obviously desperate. Suddenly he leaped from the wagon and sprinted toward the edge of the gulley. He fell once and cried out in pain. He squeezed his head between his hands and moaned. But he struggled to his feet and stumbled forward. He reached the gulley and threw himself, screaming, over the edge.

At first Tom was too shocked to move. Then he jumped down and ran to the lip of the gulley. Tobias's body lay smashed face down on the rocks forty feet below. Everything was absolutely still. Even the breeze had stopped.

Then *she* moved. The dark hump on Tobias slowly detached itself from the body. It was as if a hideous suction were being broken as each hand and foot was pulled out of Tobias. Once free she skipped off the body like a child playing hopscotch and looked up at Tom. For a split second he had the crazy thought she spoke to him.

"Wait, Tom," the high, raspy voice echoed in his mind. "I want you. I'll come for you."

A chill ran over him and made his flesh creep. The Burr Woman moved with her peculiar monkeylike agility toward the gulley wall and began to scramble up it.

Her voice kept ringing in his ears. "Wait, Tom. I want to be with you."

In less than half a minute she was well up the steep wall. The gray hair had fallen away from her dark, narrow face and Tom saw her black eyes intent on him.

Tom turned and ran. Like he'd never run before. He leaped into the wagon and whipped the horses frantically. The wagon jerked ahead and skidded down the dirt road. Panting, Tom looked back over his shoulder and saw the Burr Woman lifting herself over the edge of the gulley. She stood there a second and watched the speeding wagon. Then she began to lope after him, running like a chimp chasing a banana.

"Oh, my God," Tom said aloud. "She's coming after me."

And she was.

The Windigo

There had been six of them when they started the hunting trip. Now there were four huddled under the rock ledge as the cold autumn rain fell. The small campfire was the only comfort left them. All their weapons, food, and most of the clothes on their backs had been torn from them when the avalanche hit.

When it first came rumbling down on them the sound was gentle, as if the mountain were simply clearing its throat. But it bowled into them with such force and suddenness that Kumook's bow and arrows, which he had been clutching in his hand, were torn from him like a leaf in a tornado. Two of his companions disappeared down the mountain and a third, Mitsina, had his back broken. They had carried him down below the snow line, where the falling snow had turned to an icy rain. They couldn't have lived through the night if they hadn't found the cave.

The other two hunters and Kumook had all done their best for Mitsina, but now he lay next to the fire feverish and gasping quietly for breath. Kumook frequently bathed his face in the cold rainwater, which seemed to bring a little peace to him.

None of the men had eaten for the last four days and they were all too weak to hunt—even if they still had their weapons. Only a small skinning knife was left between them.

Kumook often shivered uncontrollably, and his head ached as if it would explode. He was sure the others felt just as weak and full of pain. His companions' faces were chalk-white. They both had sunken cheeks and hollow dark eyes.

There was nothing to be done. They were all going to die, especially if they didn't find food soon. Light Wolf had grabbed a lizard from the rock yesterday and stuffed it into his mouth before Kumook could say a word about sharing it. But then, that was Light Wolf. He wouldn't have given any of the lizard up even if Kumook had spoken.

That night Mitsina died. He finished very quietly. Kumook was bathing his face when his eyes fluttered, he groaned gently, and stopped breathing. His eyes still stared up at Kumook.

Light Wolf glanced over briefly and said, "Good. I was getting tired of all that wheezing."

Kumook hated Light Wolf at that moment.

"His lungs were full of liquid," he explained. "He was drowning."

"So?" Light Wolf sneered, staring out at the rain. "We're all drowning but we don't wheeze constantly and keep everyone else awake."

Little Bear shook his head at Kumook. "It's done now. No reason to fight over what is finished."

"The problem is what to do with the corpse," Light Wolf said. "I don't want it stinking up this small cave. And I'm too tired and cold to take it anywhere."

All three men thought for a moment. None had an answer. Finally Little Bear said, "Perhaps tomorrow. Let's sleep now and some answers may come."

For the rest of the night they huddled together, each disliking the other but needing the warmth. The corpse lay silently next to the faint fire, its pale face shimmering in the unsteady light.

The next morning everything was worse. Their hunger was a gnawing ache and weakness left them limp and breathless. The only good thing was they had plenty of water.

Light Wolf got up slowly and drank from a trickle of water running down the rock face. He put the last few dry pieces of wood on the fire. The wood caught and the cave brightened; light danced on the wall. Light Wolf sat back down but noticed that Mitsina's arm seemed to move. There, yes. It did it again. The upper arm was wiggling, slight spasmodic movements as if the muscles were trying to start up again. Suddenly the whole arm jerked and the elbow leaped an inch or so off the ground. Light Wolf jumped to his feet, trembling.

"Mitsina's come back," he croaked. "He's alive. Look," he said, pointing a shaking finger.

Too tired to care, Kumook glanced over at the body and his eyes popped open. It did move. Both legs. Mitsina's heavy thighs were irregularly jerking back and forth, up and down. Then a small dark head peeked out from underneath his thigh. The rat's pointy nose twitched and sniffed the air, then ducked back down beneath the legs.

"Ahhhggg," Little Bear cried, and pulled the body over onto its side. Underneath, ten pairs of bright, hot eyes glanced up at them. The rodents scurried in every direction. Three of them ran back into the cave and disappeared into small crevices in the rock. The other two vanished around the side of the cave entrance.

The inside of Mitsina's legs and arms had been gnawed to the bone by the rats.

The three men stared at the torn corpse, then at each other.

"Well," Light Wolf said. "What else did you expect?"

"Yes," Kumook said. "It is natural enough."

"How can you sit there and talk like that?" Little Bear said. "Have you forgotten our laws? Our religion? Those of our tribe must be respected in death. The body is not for animals to feed on. It must be kept intact until the spirit has been properly released."

"And how do you expect to do that here?" Light Wolf asked sarcastically. "We cannot burn the body.

We have barely enough dry wood to keep the fire alive."

"He's right," replied Kumook. "There is nothing we can do. All of us will share Mitsina's fate very soon."

Little Bear sat down and put his head in his hands. He knew they were right.

Suddenly Light Wolf stood up and stared at Mitsina's corpse.

"There is a way," he said quietly.

The other two looked at him. Then at Mitsina.

Kumook understood but said nothing. He just lowered his head. He didn't like the idea, but they might survive.

"Noooo," cried Little Bear suddenly. "That cannot be. We will surely be despised by the Great Spirit."

He leaped to his feet and faced Light Wolf. "Life is not worth that. I will not do it. I will not do that to my friend."

Little Bear folded his arms and turned his back on Kumook and Light Wolf.

"No one has asked you to do anything," Light Wolf said sarcastically. "You can die pure. After you go I'll even say a prayer for you."

"It is the way we can stay alive. We only have one or two more days," Kumook said.

Light Wolf laughed. "It's just meat. Meat. Take a lesson from the rats. That's where you'll be in two days if you don't."

Little Bear returned to his spot against the cave

wall and sat down. He didn't look or say a word to either of them.

"Well, how will we do it? Who goes first?" asked Light Wolf.

But they didn't have time to decide. A heavy growl rumbled. A huge grizzly bear stood on its hind legs at the cave entrance, sniffing the air and peering at the fire. It must have been ten feet tall. It came down onto its front legs and approached the fire. The three Indians retreated into the cave and pressed against the back wall. Kumook held his small knife in front of him. The bear looked at the fire for a moment, brought its nose closer, and then snorted and flicked its head back. It came forward again and sniffed Mitsina's corpse, whose head lay facing the bear. The giant bear touched the body with its nose, then its paw.

Suddenly the grizzly dug its claws into Mitsina's lifeless arm and started to pull Mitsina's body out of the cave. Its teeth clamped down on the corpse's hand and the grizzly's head jerked back like a fisherman pulling in his catch. As the body scraped along the cave floor Light Wolf and Kumook both grabbed a leg. For a moment the corpse was suspended between the bear pulling one direction and the two Indians pulling the other. The white, stiff body jiggled like a puppet trying to dance on its back. Its open, dry eyes stared. The corpse was half-out and half-in the cave, but soon the bear began to win. The Indians were so weak that they couldn't struggle against the powerful grizzly for long.

Little Bear saw the battle was going against them and leaped forward with a stick and struck the bear on the side. The grizzly shook its head angrily and growled but wouldn't release its grip on Mitsina's head. Little Bear hit the grizzly again and again, but each time the bear just growled and shook Mitsina's head back and forth, tightening its grip as its teeth sank deeper into the skull bone.

Maddened by his near starvation, by the ugly tearing apart of his friend's corpse, and his fear that he would soon be similar food for the forest, Little Bear screamed a war cry and attacked the grizzly with the stick. He beat the bear's face and muzzle, pummeled its body with his fist, kicked it, and even bit its arm. But his ferocious attack was barely noticed by the bear, who pulled even harder to take possession of Mitsina's body.

The wild struggle went on for several minutes, for the men were fighting a desperate last battle. If they could beat the bear, perhaps they had a chance for survival, perhaps they could also beat the forest and survive. But soon poor Mitsina's head yanked off in the bear's mouth and the huge grizzly tumbled backward.

The grizzly rose on its hind legs and roared its anger, rushing at the corpse again, this time slashing and cutting with its claws and fangs. Little Bear was closest as the grizzly's four long, curved claws caught him in the pit of the stomach and lifted him several feet off the ground. He landed hard against the cave wall. Kumook and Light Wolf shrank back, terrified now of the grizzly's savage counterattack. They cowered against the cave's back wall, watching in horror and fascination as the grizzly pounced possessively on Mitsina's corpse. It hunched there for a moment, front claws dug into the body's chest, fangs deeply imbedded in the shoulder. The grizzly watched the two Indians warily, then began to drag the body away.

Once the bear had Mitsina's corpse a safe distance it released its hold and bit into the waist, lifted it easily up to shoulder height, and walked off.

When Kumook and Light Wolf recovered from their fear they noticed Little Bear sitting against the wall staring straight ahead, his eyes wide and wondering. Little Bear's eyes were already glazing over and drying. Neither of them could see his chest move. He wasn't breathing anymore.

He was dead and there was no hesitation now. They both knew what had to be done in order to survive.

Light Wolf talked loud but it was Kumook that first cut into Little Bear's flesh. He set some strips aside for drying and put the rest on a flat stone heated in the fire. As it sizzled and the fat dripped into the fire Kumook's mouth watered. Light Wolf also stared hungrily at the cooking meat, but when he grabbed a piece and bit into it he immediately gagged.

He grimaced and tried again, this time succeeding in chewing and swallowing it. A moment after he finished he put his hand over his mouth and vomited. He was miserable but no matter how he tried he couldn't keep the meat down.

Kumook watched Light Wolf and wondered how he would react. His first bite surprised him. It was pleasant, even delicious. If he ignored where it came from it reminded him of bear meat. The more he ate the better it tasted. Probably because he was so starved, he thought. In the end he was stuffing the meat into his mouth. When he looked up Light Wolf was watching him in horror.

Ashamed, Kumook stopped chewing and swallowed. He wiped his greasy fingers on his stomach and arms, just as after every meal. But Light Wolf was clearly terrified for some reason.

"What's the matter?" Kumook asked. "Why do you look at me that way?"

"You like it? You find pleasure in it?" Light Wolf said, amazed.

"Yes. It didn't bother me like you."

That night the snow began to fall, and Kumook slept soundly. When he awoke Light Wolf was still asleep. He was paler than yesterday and looked gaunt. Like a corpse, Kumook thought.

Kumook ate some more meat, this time raw, because he was so hungry he didn't want to wait until it was cooked. After eating he felt strong and because they needed more firewood Kumook went out for the first time since they had taken shelter in the cave.

When he returned Light Wolf was awake. He had crept farther into the cave and sat with his back against the wall. Emaciated and frightened, he watched Kumook warily.

That day and the next, it seemed Kumook's hunger could not be satisfied. The more he ate the more he craved. Light Wolf still could not eat the meat, but he watched Kumook, more terrified of him every day.

Little Bear's corpse was soon reduced to a skeleton covered with tendons Kumook had left attached to the bones. He began sucking on them, chewing the hard gristle for hours on end. Light Wolf could not stand the endless chewing and slurping sounds Kumook made, but he was clearly too frightened to say anything.

They were now completely snowed in with the wind building drifts halfway up the cave mouth. It didn't really matter, however, there was nowhere to go even if Light Wolf had the strength. But Kumook made almost daily trips outside the cave to get wood. He beat his way through the high drifts with ease. He could have tried to get help, but the thought didn't occur to him. He wasn't sure he wanted to go anywhere.

After Little Bear's body was consumed Kumook started on the head. He devoured it with the same gusto and pleasure as the rest of Little Bear.

The morning after he had finished off Little Bear, Kumook awoke to find Light Wolf gone. For some reason he wasn't surprised. Deep inside himself he seemed to have known it was coming. He immediately started after Light Wolf.

The trail through the snow was easy to follow and he caught up with him in an hour. He saw Light Wolf struggling to get down a steep decline and called his name. Light Wolf looked over his shoulder and cried out in alarm, "No. No. Go away. Leave me alone."

Light Wolf began to run frantically, stumbling every few steps in his haste to get away. Kumook jumped on him and they fell into the snow. Light Wolf's face was stricken with panic. He raised his hands to ward off Kumook.

Kumook held him down and looked into his face.

"Calm down," he said. "What's the matter? Why did you leave me like that, Light Wolf?"

Light Wolf was shocked. "You don't know yet? You don't see it? You're a *Windigo!* A flesh-eater. You even look different, you've become more beast than man. You'll never be able to stop now. You will never die, but never again will you crave anything as much as human flesh.

"Please," Light Wolf pleaded. "Let me go. If we've ever been friends, let me go. I'd rather die out here in the forest than be food for you."

Kumook suddenly realized Light Wolf was right. There was a craving in him. He had felt it building and he knew now he'd eat human flesh again even if he didn't have to. There was no chioce. In fact, Light Wolf was also right to run away, for while Kumook had never thought about it consciously, he was surely going to eat him.

Suddenly Kumook was free. The realization that he didn't care about Light Wolf at all, except as food, freed him forever. He struck Light Wolf in the face with his fist. Light Wolf's eyes rolled up in his head and he groaned.

"No, oh, no. Not like this," he moaned, shaking his head back and forth.

Kumook struck him again and again until finally Light Wolf lay still. He felt saliva already flooding his mouth. Kumook threw him over his shoulder and started back to the cave. It was now his home. There was no reason to go back to the tribe. He could wait here for others to come into the mountains.

The Snake Woman of Wales

A shoemaker in the Welsh village of Taff married a widow named Elsie Venner for her money. Since there was little love between them they soon quarreled. Sometimes the fights became so violent that the neighbors whispered among themselves how strange that neither of them appeared to have any bruises or signs of fighting.

The fights went on night after night. Loud cries and deep groans could be heard all night long from the shoemaker's house. One neighbor, an inquisitive fellow named Frank Wendell, became so curious that he snuck into the shoemaker's house and hid in a loft over the kitchen. The fighting went on that night as it had for so many before. But Wendell would not tell anyone what he had seen, even though most people in Taff knew he had actually witnessed the strange couple fighting. One rumor spread around that he had been discovered by the couple and bribed to say nothing.

The village came to accept the violent marriage between the shoemaker and the widow and said little—until the shoemaker began to appear ill. He grew ever thinner and weaker, and after several months he died. No marks were found on his body but the doctor who tended him during his last illness declared that he had died from the poisonous stings of a serpent.

The doctor's accusation frightened and disturbed the village. How could it be true? No snakes had been discovered in the village. The doctor must be mistaken, everyone whispered, for no one wanted to believe a snake spirit was to blame.

It was then Frank Wendell visited the doctor and told his own story. When he had hidden in the shoemaker's loft, what he had seen was so horrible that he didn't think anyone would believe him. The woman, Wendell claimed, was a snake demon. As soon as angry words passed between husband and wife, Elsie assumed the shape of a serpent from her shoulders upward. Her serpent's head struck the man time and again. When the man was faint and weakened she pierced him with her fangs and sucked his blood until he fell to the floor unconscious. The two men's stories taken together carried enough weight so that Elsie was soon feared and avoided by the people of Taff.

One night Elsie's servant came to both Wendell's and the doctor's homes to invite them to dinner so she could explain her side of the controversy. At first they hesitated but eventually agreed because they didn't want to appear frightened of a lone woman.

Elsie, who was a tall, thin woman with graying hair, had prepared a grand meal for them. After they had eaten she served them drinks in memory of her departed husband. As soon as they had swallowed the drinks both men's eyesight blurred and their heads seemed to spin. As they sank into unconsciousness they saw Elsie Venner's face dissolve in a rush of scales that seemed to flood down from her scalp. Her eyes sank into her head and her upper and lower jaws pushed forward into a hard snout. The last thing they saw before the light disappeared from their minds was the long, red tongue flickering at them as she struck toward their necks.

Frank Wendell awoke in the churchyard, flat on his back. His head ached so terribly he couldn't move. His mouth tasted like metal and his arms and legs didn't obey his commands to move. So he lay there staring up into the branches of a tree until he heard voices. Straining every muscle he managed to lift his hand slightly. A groan somehow escaped despite the horrible exhaustion that made him think he was dying.

The children who were frightening each other by playing in the cemetery were startled for real by the groan coming from behind the bushes and tombstones. Screaming, they all fled the place in seconds, leaving the helpless man crying silently.

But they told their story and police came shortly after and found Wendell's paralyzed body. He was barely alive and was taken to the hospital where he was treated for snakebite. The doctor was dead, his eyes wide open in horror. Puncture wounds from snake bites were found all over his face and neck. Wendell, the doctors said, would also have died within a few hours if he had not been found.

Elsie Venner was never seen again but every time a snake appears near Taff it is said to be "the old snake woman."

Nevillon's Toad

Nevillon was one of those men you see on the street and everyone whispers, "Look at the weirdo." He was tall and angular, everything about him had sharp angles including his nose, which was long and sharp. He always dressed in black, and those who saw him regularly over the years swore that it was the *same* black jacket and baggy pants.

In one way those frightened by Nevillon were right. He had little affection for people. In fact, he disliked every living thing except cats. Nevillon lived in a small room atop a run-down brownstone which he shared with his twenty-three cats. His "family" was soon to expand because some of the females were about to give birth.

But the thing all these people who laughed at Nevillon didn't realize was that he was truly a magician and alchemist. Nevillon wasn't interested in transforming lead into gold, he had labored for thirty years to bring the nonliving into life. He wanted to create life from nothing. And he was close. That very night he planned his final experiment. His only problem was *what* to create. He didn't like people, even if they would be his own creation. Besides, they were too dangerous, too difficult to control. He didn't want to deal with any living thing that was even close to being human.

He thought of making a cat. But even though they were gentle, independent creatures, it would be... well... excessive to make another when he already had twenty-three. So he debated for days. What to make? What was the thing furthest from human? A reptile? They were too slinky and slimy. He thought and thought and finally decided on a toad. It was alive and nonhuman. And it was gay. It hopped a lot and this idea pleased Nevillon.

Nevillon worked hard all through the night and just before dawn he finished. The giant toad, which was almost the size of a large dog, was made mostly from lead and leather. It lay on the table softly pulsing, its large round belly moving in and out rhythmically as it breathed.

Nevillon was pleased but very tired. Preparing the many ingredients and performing the complicated rituals had exhausted him. He lay down to sleep as the sun came up. How appropriate, he thought, a new day and a new life. This must be the way God felt.

When he awoke it was night again. He leaped out of bed, lit the lamp, and went quickly to his creation. The giant toad had sprouted short pale blue hair all over its leather hide. Something must have gone wrong, Nevillon thought. He hadn't planned on any hair. Oh, well, no harm done. In fact, it looked quite pretty.

It was awake and its round fish eyes glanced furtively around the room. They paused on Nevillon and the two stared at each other. After a moment it opened its mouth and croaked hoarsely at Nevillon, almost like a baby's first cry.

Nevillon was delighted and slapped his thigh several times, which he always did when he was happy. "Oh my, oh my," he kept repeating ecstatically. "I've done it. I've done it."

The huge toad seemed to catch his enthusiasm and began croaking and hopping around the room. The cats began hissing and running in all directions, frightened of the big blue toad and its wild jumping. They hid under the tables and leaped up to the top of chests and shelves, the hair on their arched backs straight up along their spines.

At first Nevillon was so pleased he had created life that the noise and turmoil didn't bother him. But in a few days his natural desire for quiet returned and he became nervous and irritable. He went out of the house more often, walking the city alone late at night. Whenever anyone dared to speak to the forbidding dark figure he snapped at them to leave him alone.

In a few days the constant croaking of the blue toad was driving him crazy. He couldn't bear to destroy his creation but he had to do something, so he built a large box and stuffed the toad in it. The toad continued to croak and hop about inside the box, which made it bounce around the room crazily. When the box suddenly bounced off the table and crushed one of Nevillon's cats, he had had enough. He cut a hole in the floor, put the box in it, and replaced the floorboards. The toad was quiet for a time and then began to croak and kick under the floor. The croaking was faint but its kicking was so powerful the floor thumped and bounced visibly.

Within a week however, Nevillon's pride got the better of him and he took the toad out of its box to admire his handiwork. He was so pleased that even with the irritating croaking he let the creature out more and more often. After all, he told himself, he could still hear it under the floorboards anyway. So why not enjoy looking at his creation? One shouldn't hide away something as beautiful as a giant blue toad.

One day when he returned from his daily walk all the cats were huddled against the apartment wall, hissing at the toad. Their hair was stiff and their eyes full of fear. The huge blue toad was puffed out and squatted in the center of the room watching the cats, his head swinging back and forth surveying them like a drill sergeant.

"What is going on here?" bellowed Nevillon. "Why can't you all get along?"

Nevillon paced up and down the apartment as the cats slinked away to find hiding places. The toad seemed to smirk as he watched their frightened scurrying.

"I can't live like this," exploded Nevillon. "I hate

confusion. I will not have this chaos in my house. Do you hear?" he screamed at them all.

"And you, Toad," he yelled, turning on the blue monster still squatting possessively in the middle of the room. "I don't know what to do with you. Ever since you arrived the whole place has been crazy."

Nevillon threw himself into his favorite chair and put his head in his hands. "I never should have created it," he moaned. "But what can I do now? I can't destroy it. It would be like killing a part of myself."

Nevillon's head began to ache so he went to bed. Perhaps he'd find an answer tomorrow.

When he awoke the sun was just setting. He lit his lamp and prepared breakfast for himself and the cats, still trying to figure a way out of his dilemma. It didn't occur to him to make anything for the toad, for he couldn't imagine it wanting to eat. And indeed the blue toad sat passively and watched as Nevillon and the cats ate.

But something else was bothering Nevillon. It wasn't just his problem about what to do with the toad. He couldn't put his finger on it, but there was something wrong. He looked around the room. Everything was in order. His books and manuscripts were all right. His scientific equipment was just where he left it. Then it occurred to him. There were fewer cats. Yes, that was it. The number definitely seemed smaller. He quickly counted them as they ate. Nineteen. Strange, he was sure there had been twenty-three. Had some left? That happened sometimes. A cat would get restless and just disappear. Go wandering off into the world looking for new adventure, is the way Nevillon put it. It was one of the things he loved most about cats—their marvelous independence. But he'd never had four leave all at once. Perhaps the toad had frightened them off? That was probably the answer. And so he put the mystery of the missing cats out of his mind.

Later that night he was reading in his chair and happened to look up at the blue toad. It was hunched over in a corner of the room, its great bellows throat puffing in and out. It made a peculiar gurgling sound, like it was clearing its throat. Then it stopped, was absolutely still. Not a muscle twitched. Even its eyes stopped their constant rolling.

Nevillon was amused and fascinated by the toad's strange behavior and watched it clinically. Suddenly, almost faster than Nevillon's eye could follow, its wide mouth opened and a long black tongue snapped out and caught a cat around the neck. The cat shrieked but it was yanked back into the toad's gaping mouth before it could even begin to struggle. The toad snapped its mouth a few times, as if smacking its lips, swallowed, and the cat was gone. A small tip of its tail lingered in the toad's mouth.

Nevillon sat up in horror and watched as the toad's stomach bulged and pulsed with the cat's struggle to get out. The blue toad looked over at Nevillon with—if it was possible—a satisfied grin on its face. Its thick black tongue came out and licked around its mouth. The cat's tail disappeared.

Only a few stray hairs clung to its chops.

"Oh, my Lord," Nevillon groaned. "Oh, my Lord. What have I done?"

Now he knew. The missing cats had been food for the blue toad. Nevillon broke down and wept as the toad hopped over and looked up at him like a concerned puppy. It croaked once or twice in sympathy with its unhappy master. Then, getting no response, it went back to hunting the cats. It hopped over to the table and peered under it. But the cats had learned already and taken to the higher ground. He looked under the old piano, the chairs, the stove, and dressers. Nothing. All the cats were balefully watching the blue monster from high on the book shelves. Some were even clinging to the curtains near the ceiling, hanging on with their claws. They all glared at the terrible pale blue thing that had come into their home.

Nevillon was at his wit's end. He loved his cats, who had been his only companions for years. But he was deeply and mysteriously tied to his creation. He just couldn't bring himself to kill it. There must be another way. Nevillon sat in his chair thinking. Thinking. Thinking. Nothing came and in despair he almost gave up and was going to kill the toad when he got an idea.

"Of course," he cursed at himself. It was so obvious. Why hadn't he thought of it before?

Nevillon jumped up, threw on his coat, and went out. If the toad was hungry, he would feed it. He had neglected to feed it, so naturally it had turned to the only food there—the cats. But, he chuckled to himself, if he kept it stuffed and well-fed the problem would be solved.

Nevillon experimented. First he bought beef. The toad rejected it. Then he tried lamb. No good. Chicken. Veal. Duck. Nothing worked. The toad sniffed the offerings, even once or twice flicked its tongue to taste the food but finally rejected it all. It seemed to like live food only.

Whenever Nevillon came home he noticed there were fewer and fewer cats. They were going fast and he was distraught. More miserable than he'd ever been in his life. But every time he pushed himself to the edge and convinced himself that he must kill the toad he hesitated and went into a long internal conversation. He always managed to talk himself out of it. He also couldn't figure out how the toad was getting the cats. He'd hoped that once they stayed up on the shelves the toad couldn't get to them. And indeed, they were terrified of the toad and kept well out of its reach. They spent all their time near the ceiling. Nevillon even had to put their food dishes up on a shelf before they'd eat.

There were only nine cats remaining. And Nevillon had a special problem. Two females were about to give birth. They couldn't very well do it on a shelf near the ceiling, so Nevillon built a wooden box with small slats the cats could squeeze in and out of. He put the females in the box when their time came and watched over them carefully until the kittens were born.

The toad was intrigued by the box and watched it for hours on end. But Nevillon had built it strong and was confident it could keep the mothers and kittens safe.

He was wrong. One night when he returned from his walk the box was crushed and the kittens were gone. The mothers were howling in rage and fear on the top bookshelves. The toad was smiling up at them licking its mouth. It croaked at Nevillon happily when he came in the door.

Nevillon wept again that night. There were only a few cats left now. The toad was killing them at a fast rate, several every day. How it was getting them down from their high perches Nevillon couldn't understand. Then one night as he was working on an experiment he heard a squeal and looked up. One cat was being swallowed and the toad was hopping back and forth under the bookshelves, its eyes intent on another cat that scurried desperately over the books and shelves. Suddenly the toad's thick black tongue shot out. It reached all the way to the ceiling, snapped the cat in the face with its sticky end and pulled the spitting, hissing animal back into its mouth. It was all over in a second.

Nevillon was stunned. He hadn't created a tongue that long. The toad was changing, continuing to alter its body. Its body was adapting to life. Amazed, Nevillon watched the toad with fascination. Now he understood many things. The toad was continuing to evolve and for that it needed food. He had only started the process of life, but once started it went its own way.

The toad hopped over to Nevillon and rubbed its head on his leg and croaked several times. After a moment Nevillon understood. It wanted more food. That had been the last cat.

When Nevillon realized all his cats had been eaten by the blue toad he became angry and hysterical.

"I don't care how fascinating a creation you are!" Nevillon shouted at the toad. "You've eaten my cats and I'll never forgive you for that."

Nevillon sank into a depressed silence. He wouldn't talk to the toad, he wouldn't even talk to himself. Then one night the following week it happened. He was sitting at the table writing when a sharp pain shot through his leg. The toad had wrapped its sticky tongue around his calf. Nevillon jumped up and screamed.

"Let go, let go, you little blue monster!"

He slapped the toad's tongue. It was hot and sticky and enormously powerful. It felt like a hot steel band around his leg. The toad tugged on his leg and slowly pulled Nevillon toward it. Nevillon grabbed a broom and began beating the toad on the head. He hit it over and over again until finally the toad released his leg. His calf was circled with a wide red welt. Small drops of blood trickled down his skin into his shoe.

Nevillon limped to the bathroom and put some alcohol and a bandage on his leg, then returned to the living room. He was livid with anger. He sat in his chair and regarded the toad, who looked mildly back at him. The broom handle had broken but Nevillon clutched a large piece protectively as he considered what to do with the toad. He couldn't even sleep safely with it. If that steel tongue ever got around his neck, he'd be finished before he could defend himself.

Then it came clear to him. Perfect justice. He wouldn't even have to destroy the toad himself. He would start tonight. He had everything he needed. It would take him all night but by morning it would be over. He would make some cats. Many, many cats to replace those the blue toad had eaten. He smiled.

"And then we'll see," Nevillon said aloud as the toad hopped over to him, rubbed its head on his leg, and croaked.

The Beast of Csejthe Castle

Katalin had never been so excited. She had always wanted to leave the small, boring village and live in a great castle among grand ladies and lords. She and her twin sister had argued many times, for Ilona didn't care about castles and kings and grand living. Kata, as her family called her, had begged Ilona to go with her to serve the Countess Bathory. She dreamed nightly that she and Ilona would one day serve the Lady Bathory as dresser and seamstress. Only the strange dwarf Janos Ujvary, who served the Lady and had told her mother about the work in the castle, made her uncomfortable. He was so ugly. And Kata only liked beautiful things.

Countess Bathory was one of the richest and most powerful persons in the whole kingdom. Her cousin was Prime Minister of Hungary, men in her family were famous heroes and generals in the army. Her family ruled almost half the country. The thought of all that power and wealth made Kata giddy and she constantly bombarded Ilona with stories of what living in such luxury would be like. To Kata's delight she finally gave in and they prepared to leave home.

The morning the girls left for Csejthe Castle, the Countess's ancestral home, the sky was bright and clear. The trip was supposed to take two days in a horse-drawn carriage. But the two days turned into four when the carriage broke a wheel over rough dirt roads and they waited in a filthy inn for its repair.

The carriage was stuffy and dust-filled, and they eventually arrived covered in grime, with aching backs, hungry and thirsty. But the sight of Csejthe Castle made them forget their pain. It was breathtaking, sitting majestically on a hill high above the surrounding valley, with the small village pressed beneath its massive stone walls.

The castle was the grandest they had ever seen, even in books and paintings. But they had little time to appreciate it, for as soon as the carriage pulled up to the entrance a heavyset woman with a fat, round face and rouged-red cheeks came out. She was almost totally bald and her full lips were surrounded by scraggly, long black hairs. In fact, she looked just like a fat, bald man with a thin beard. She was the most ugly woman either girl had ever seen. Her name was Dorka Szentes.

The sisters were immediately frightened by this brusque, ugly woman who grabbed their arms and shuttled them into the servants' quarters.

But even Dorka's short-tempered comments couldn't dampen Kata's enthusiasm. She was thrilled by the vast halls, the complicated and brightly colored tapestries and paintings on the walls. Almost her whole village could fit into the single great hall. At one point Kata stopped to gape openmouthed at a huge painting of the castle's mistress.

"Oh, Ilona," Kata said. "She is so beautiful. I've never seen anyone so beautiful. She must be a wonderful person for God to have made her so pretty."

Dorka suddenly grabbed Kata's shoulder in a viselike grip and squeezed hard until she cried out in pain.

"There," Dorka said in her deep male voice. "That will show you the way things are here, child. Don't speak until you're spoken to. Don't stop unless you're ordered to. Do exactly what you're told or you'll suffer."

Dorka smiled thinly at the girls and pushed them through a door into a long hall with a series of rooms, one of which they were given as their own. Dorka quickly told them the house rules and left.

Kata had a sore shoulder, but even Dorka's crude lesson in the great hall didn't bother her. She was still wide-eyed with excitement. So what if she had to put up with the old witch in order to stay in this magnificent castle? If that was the price, she would gladly pay it.

Ilona, however, was frightened by Dorka's quick violence and wanted to go home right away. Kata laughed and told her to ignore ugly old Dorka. They worked for the Lady Elisabeth Bathory, and any woman so beautiful and grand would be kind and surely protect them.

At dinner in the kitchen that evening they met

another servant who had arrived only several days before. Sitkey was a thin girl who had been hired from far away in the Hungarian lowlands and had traveled for over a month to reach the castle.

Sitkey's face was pale and her expression sad. At first she didn't say much and Kata's open joy at being in the castle seemed to make Sitkey even sadder. Finally the frail girl reached across the table and touched Kata's hand and whispered intensely.

"Please, please, don't talk so. This is not a happy place. I have only been here a few days, yet it seems months. Every night there is—"

Sitkey suddenly stopped and sat up straight in her chair, her lips pressed tightly together. Dorka had entered the kitchen behind Kata and Ilona.

The fat woman barely glanced at them as she stomped through the kitchen and out a back door. Sitkey began trembling and then began to weep softly.

Kata and Ilona went to her and stroked her.

"What is it, Sitkey? What's the matter?" they said gently. "Can we help?"

"No, no. Just leave me alone."

Sitkey jumped up from her chair and ran out of the room. Her food had not been touched. That was the last time Kata or Ilona ever saw Sitkey.

Late that night the girls were awakened by screams. At first their sleep-drugged brains couldn't identify the sound. Owls screeching? Old doors in the castle creaking open and shut? Window shutters groaning in the wind? Then almost simultaneously both girls recognized that they were human screams.

"Mother in heaven," Ilona whispered. "What is that?"

"I don't know," Kata whispered back. "Someone must be hurt. Perhaps an accident?"

But both girls knew the screaming was no accident. It was too constant and had been going on for too long.

"I'll find out," Kata said, getting out of bed.

"No, no. Don't leave me," Ilona begged. "I don't want to stay here alone."

"All right. Come with me," Kata said and went to the door.

The long hallway was empty and black. Not a light anywhere. The girls felt their way along the hall to the kitchen. It was empty. Kata remembered a small lamp had been on the counter. She found it after a minute of groping in the dark. Then she found some matches in a drawer and lit it. The faint glow it shed was comforting and the girls followed the sound of the screams to the back door Dorka had used that afternoon.

Steep steps led down into the dark. The lamp showed them only a few steps at a time. Beyond that was a wall of blackness. But the screams were definitely coming from somewhere in the dark pit below them.

They crept deeper into the recesses below the castle and the screams grew louder and louder. The terrible sounds echoed up the stairwell and sent chills running over them. They had gone down at least a hundred steps when suddenly the screams stopped. The girls clutched each other and waited. A door clanged loudly far beneath them and voices drifted up.

"Lift up, I said," one gruff voice ordered. "Get her legs."

"Don't tell me what to do," another answered. "You carry her. I've done all the work tonight."

Kata and Ilona recognized two male and two female voices as the arguing went on for several minutes. Then a commanding female voice cut them off.

"Stop this. It's getting late. The bath must be ready in half an hour. Four o'clock. Not one minute later or you'll all pay."

The other voices immediately stopped. A door slammed. Silence. And then the arguing began again.

"Get upstairs now. First thing. The rest can wait."

"But the body..."

"No arguing," said a voice that sounded like Dorka's. "You heard the orders."

Steps echoed as someone began climbing the stairs toward Kata and Ilona. The girls turned and scrambled up the stairs as fast as their legs could go. The steps behind them seemed to get closer and the girls thought they would never reach the kitchen door. But in a moment they burst out into the kitchen and scurried for their room. Panting they closed their bedroom door and leaned against it, trembling.

Steps echoed down the long hall outside their room and Kata pressed a finger to her lips and opened the door a crack. Janos the dwarf and another man were each carrying two large buckets full to the brim with a dark liquid. The two men bumped into each other in the narrow hall and some of the thick liquid slopped onto the floor. They ignored it and hurried on.

Kata closed the door and leaned against it. Neither girl spoke for a minute; they just stared at each other, their eyes wide with fear. Then Ilona said, "I don't like this. I want to go home."

Kata put her arm around Ilona. "It's probably nothing bad. Just some workmen repairing something downstairs. I bet that's all it is."

"It scares me," Ilona said, her voice trembling. "And I don't want to stay."

Ilona went to her bed and began to sob. "I want to go home. I want to go home."

Kata caressed her sister's blond head and said gently, "All right, all right. We'll tell them tomorrow we can't work here."

The girls slept fitfully the rest of the night, huddled together on one bed.

The next morning they got dressed and started toward the kitchen for breakfast. The horror of the night screams were distant, if not forgotten. But everything rushed back when they saw the bloody stains on the floor outside their room.

Just then the breakfast bell rang and other servants came out of their rooms. As they passed, Kata pointed to the spot on the floor, asking if anyone knew what it was. No one answered Kata. Only Sara, another of Lady Bathory's seamstresses, paused long enough to whisper.

"Better be quiet. Stop asking questions."

"But the screams last night—" Kata said.

"Forget the screams," Sara replied quickly, and then she was gone into the kitchen.

Kata and Ilona were badly frightened and asked to see Dorka. Now they both wanted to go home. Later that morning Dorka called for them. The two girls stood in front of the fat woman and explained there had been a mistake and that they couldn't take the jobs. They wanted to go home.

Dorka listened to them and when they had finished she laughed. The sound echoed in the big stone room.

"You simpletons," she said. "You don't understand anything, do you. Shall I tell you something? You were brought here because you're strong and healthy. You are a gift to the Lady Elisabeth. You're not going home. Not today, not tomorrow. Not ever."

Dorka smiled bleakly and stood up. She towered over the girls.

"Do you understand now?" she said roughly. She pulled a long cord that hung down the wall. Almost immediately, as if they'd been waiting outside the door, Janos the dwarf and another man came in.

"Take them downstairs," Dorka ordered.

The big man grabbed the girls by the hair and pulled them to a large wooden door. Janos followed, making sure they didn't try to escape. The door led to another set of steps that dropped steeply down under the castle. At the bottom were catacombs that ended at an enormous square room.

At first the stunned girls didn't grasp what was happening. But the evil in the room overwhelmed them. Along one wall sets of chains were attached to metal rings.

Janos and a square, powerful peasant named

Ficzko clamped heavy, cold iron cuffs on the girls' wrists. This was too much for the frightened girls, and they began to sob and scream for mercy. They pleaded with Ficzko and Janos to let them go. They had done nothing wrong and there was no reason to punish them.

Janos listened to their hysterical cries and when they finally began to calm down he said softly, "You don't understand, young ladies. It doesn't matter whether you've done anything wrong or not. You've been brought here by order of her Ladyship and there is nothing anyone can do about it."

Janos paused a moment. He didn't really know what to say in order to make the girls' coming ordeal less painful. There was nothing he could do. The Countess could kill him at any time like a gnat, even just for a whim.

"You are not the first," he said, looking up at the girls.

"You talk too much," Ficzko said bluntly in his thick voice.

Both men turned and left through the same door. The girls continued to cry until they became hoarse and their sobs turned into little whimpers of fear.

Janos hated this part of his job. He hated the Countess Bathory as well, but he feared her more. Her power was so great she could defy King Matthias himself and probably get away with it. He had thought many times of running away, but there was no place in all Hungary he could go without the Countess finding him.

Every night he had nightmares filled with the screams of her victims.

It was hard for Janos sometimes to believe that the horror he lived with daily was real. He had been in the castle for too long.

His task tonight would be easier. He only had to spy on Pastor Poniken, who had been preaching against the Countess. He wouldn't dare use her name in his sermons, but bodies found drained of blood under the castle walls had started the rumors about the Countess all over again.

Pastor Poniken's church was a small wooden building at the end of the village's cobblestoned main street. When Janos arrived the pastor was in full cry against the ungodly people who practice black magic. Janos slipped into the back of the church and stood beside some drapes that hung along the back wall. He had a good memory and would report everything the pastor said to the Countess.

Janos left before the service ended. He had heard enough. He returned to the castle and went directly to Lady Elisabeth's bedroom. He entered through a secret tunnel that ran behind the castle walls. Before he opened the panel into her room he knocked quietly. Her melodious voice answered.

The room was encased in shadows and Janos knew she was in her "dark corner," where she always sat when she didn't have on her rouge and powders. Every year she became more desperate to stop aging. But even with all the oils and ointments, the magic incantations, and the ghastly baths, her face sagged with heavy lines. Nothing fazed this obsession to stay young. If something didn't work she merely changed the rituals. Recently she had been attempting to invoke the cat god Isten. There was nothing she wouldn't try, no matter how vile or corrupt. And her faith in black magic never wavered.

"Well," she said from her dark corner, "was it true? Is the pastor against me?"

"Yes, my Lady," Janos said. "He doesn't dare speak your name, but his message is clear."

Janos repeated the sermon to her. When he had finished her voice became hard and menacing.

"Go to the feeding room and wait. I will be there shortly."

This is what he had expected—and dreaded. Of all the nasty jobs he had, nothing frightened and repulsed him as much as the feeding of the cats.

The feeding room stank of cats. Just to walk into the large, cold room made him sick to his stomach. But more than anything he dreaded when the cats came. Just the thought made him nervous. He worked swiftly to get everything ready. He took the bowls of food from the cooler and placed them on the large table in the center of the room.

He didn't hear her enter but smelled her heavy perfume.

"Is everything prepared?" she asked.

"Yes, my Lady," he answered.

"Then let's begin."

The Countess went to the altar, lit the incense, and knelt. Her prayer was silent but Janos felt its power immediately. The room chilled where there was no breeze. The incense mixed with her heavy perfume made his head swim. Janos knew she was invoking her demon familiar, Isten.

The cats seemed to appear magically. Suddenly—from holes in the walls, under tables and chairs, behind the curtains—they came and filled the room. Outside the windows faces suddenly appeared, mouths moving silently in mute cries to get in. They filled every window and scratched, their claws grating on the glass. It was part of Janos's job to open the windows, and he ran to let them in. As he opened the latches dozens of cats of every description poured into the room. None made any sound once they were inside except a throaty purr that grew to a vibrating, soft rumble as their number increased.

Soon there were over a hundred cats gathered around the Countess's feet, tails twitching, rubbing against her skirts, looking up at her with bright, hungry eyes. She stopped her chanting, went to the table, and with both hands took one of the several huge bowls of vile food and placed it at her feet. She repeated the ritual and after the bowls had been placed on the floor Elisabeth and Janos watched in silence. The only sound was the slurping of the cats' tongues, the only movement the irregular switching of their tails, like a wheat field of furry stalks caressing the air.

The Countess slowly made her way through the carpeting of cats to the altar, which was covered with a scarlet cloth and richly embroidered with demons and cats carrying off sacrificial victims. She knelt again before the altar and began a soft, murmuring song in Latin.

"Isten," she pleaded. "Hear my call and help me. Isten, I am in danger. You are supreme commander of all cats. Send me ninety-nine warrior cats. Send me avenging cats. Tell them to gather from wherever they may be, on mountains, rivers, and seas. Order the avenging ninety-nine to come to me and bite the heart of Pastor Poniken. Order them to bite the heart of King Matthias who now listens to my enemies. Order them to bite the heart of my cousin, Count Thurzo, the Prime Minister. Command them to claw and bite the Pastor Poniken who preaches against me.

"Oh, hear my call, dark forces. Hear me, Isten, Black Commander of my demons."

The incantation went on and on. The room seemed to fill with an evil presence. The cats purred. As the Countess's repetitive prayer grew louder and more fierce the cats stopped eating and looked up. Their shining eyes focused on her just as if they understood what she was saying.

Several times during the feeding ritual a cat would press against Janos. And tonight a black-and-white monster lifted itself on its hind legs and placed its front paws, claws extended, on his shoulders. He was so short they stood tensely eye to eye. Inches from his face, it licked its jowls. Janos began trembling with anxiety. He hated cats. Hated them more than anything in the world. Sweat poured off him.

Then, as abruptly as it had come, the cat dropped to the floor and returned to its meal. Shaking like a leaf Janos crept to a corner and climbed up on a chair. He pressed his back against the wall. Tears ran down his face. One day this would drive him mad.

* * *

Pastor Poniken had the habit of reading in his den before going to bed. He liked to review the day's events and think through his sermons. The sermon tonight had been good. It had aroused the fear of the people. The Countess had gone too far, but her power was immense. Her relatives were so numerous that anyone who publicly even embarrassed her would probably be killed.

He had gone as far as he could tonight. Only two paths lay open to him. One was the note left by his predecessor detailing his suspicions about the Countess. The other was the discovery of two bodies in the woods. Their identity was clearly established. They were of noble birth. Girls from powerful and respected families who had been told that their daughters had died of disease and been given a Christian burial. He could now prove that was a lie and raise the anger of other nobles against the Countess. Tomorrow he planned to send all the evidence to these families, with copies to King Matthias.

Suddenly he heard the howling of cats. It seemed to be coming from the upper floor of the house. Puzzled, he got up and went to the door to call his servant.

"Jano. Jano. Come here."

In a moment the small man appeared in his nightshirt. He was puffing.

"Listen, Jano. Don't wake up my wife. I don't want to trouble her, but I hear some cats in the house. Or perhaps they're outside. Go and see what it is. If there are any cats, kill them. Don't be afraid, just do as I say."

The pastor returned to his study and opened a window. In a moment he saw Jano scuffling along in his slippers, a large stick in his hand. He disappeared into the night shadows at the edge of the house. There was silence for a time, then a loud cry, the wild smack of beating wood, and silence.

The pastor leaned out of the window and called, "Jano. Jano, where are you? Answer me."

Silence. Only the occasional mewing of cats filtered through the darkness.

Pastor Poniken was a small man, but with his belief in God he feared little. In fact, his fear of death was not for anything other than he might not have enough time to finish his work. Not enough time to clean the land of Countess Bathory.

He called Jano several more times and still there was no response. He slipped on his jacket and went downstairs. A flood of cats surged into the house as soon as he opened the door. They spit and hissed and clawed his legs and bit his feet. Some began to claw his clothes and hands. Others leaped and clung to his chest, biting into his jacket.

Stunned by the suddenness of the attack, the pastor fell back into the hallway. He managed to keep his feet. Somewhere in his mind he realized that if he fell to the ground he was a dead man. So he struggled to stay upright at all costs. His hand touched the umbrella rack and he grasped his walking stick. He began to beat the cats, yelling at the top of his lungs.

"You devils go to hell. Leave this place, in the name of Jesus Christ."

His fear lent strength to him and he swung the

stick again and again. He felt it crush bone and heard the cats howl in pain. But still they came. He felt himself weaken, his head spun, and his eyes clouded. He began to pray and repeated the Lord's Prayer as he struck out at the cats with his last remaining strength.

Then suddenly there was help. Jano was next to him screaming and beating at the cats. Other servants ran forward and joined them. Fur and screams filled the room until Jano managed to close the front door. Then all the cats still in the house fled. They disappeared into other rooms, up the stairs, down into the cellar, and out windows.

The pastor fell to his knees. "My God, my God. Thank you. Thank you," he gasped as he tried to catch his breath. The distant howling of cats could still be faintly heard.

As soon as he was able the pastor ordered the house searched for any remaining cats. Every room was to be sanctified, to be exorcised, to be sprinkled with holy water that very night. Immediately. A cross was hung on the front door and on each window.

When the doctor came and cared for the many wounds of Pastor Poniken and his servants he couldn't believe his eyes. They were covered with dozens and dozens, perhaps hundreds, of bites and scratches. Some of the cuts needed stitches and the doctor worked until morning patching and sewing the wounds. The pastor stayed up the rest of the night in his study working. He wrote the letters to the families of the dead girls and to King Matthias. He arranged his personal affairs in case he didn't survive the trials and difficulties of the next few days. But one way or another it would be over. Either he would die or the Countess Bathory's career would be finished.

Kata and Ilona spent the night and the next day chained to the wall. They had cried themselves out. There were no more tears left in them. Their mouths and lips were parched. Distant sounds echoed through the room just before the large metal door to the torture chamber swung open and Dorka, followed by Janos, Ficzko, another woman, and the Countess, came in. The Countess was still beautiful even though she was in her late forties. Her face was round and delicate, with wide, innocent eyes. But her beauty was ruined by heavy makeup and rouge. Dorka smiled at the girls, her eyes cold.

"Well, well. Now it is your turn," she said softly to them. All eyes in the room were on Dorka and the two girls.

Dorka waddled to a large metal winch with a handle attached to it. She disconnected the winch and, by turning the handle, lowered a metal cage down from the ceiling. It was a square cage with a small door just large enough for a normal-sized person to enter. But the floor of the cage was covered with spikes.

Dorka unchained Ilona. Kata was screaming and pleading, and Ilona was sobbing uncontrollably, when the door burst open and people flooded into the room.

At first there was stunned silence. Count Thurzo, the Lord Palatine and cousin to Lady Bathory, stared in horror at the scene.

"My God," he said in a trembling voice. "I didn't want to believe it."

Pastor Poniken and the bailiff, Gaspar Kardos, also stood in shocked silence. Pastor Poniken said a prayer silently, his lips barely moving. The bailiff finally found his voice and cursed out loud. He turned to his men.

"Search the place. Everything. I want every nook and cranny looked into. Not an inch overlooked. Do you understand?"

His men ran off with lanterns held high in front of them.

Countess Bathory had recovered from her surprise and became indignant.

"What are you doing in my house? This is unforgivable. Bailiff, march these people out of here. And as for you, cousin," she said to the Count, "I hope you have a good explanation for this intrusion."

The Count stared at her. "You must be mad to ask for an explanation."

Count Thurzo stiffened and visibly tried to gain control of himself. "All right. This is so beastly, so barbaric and horrible, I don't want to do something I'll be sorry for."

The Count walked over to Countess Bathory. "You want an explanation. Fine. You are found out. It is as simple as that. Your incomprehensible, murderous life is exposed. I have been petitioned by King Matthias to travel here and check the allegations and rumors about your magic practices. On my way I met Pastor Poniken's messenger, who was riding to the King with documentation of your crimes. I went immediately to the pastor's home and we arranged to bring the bailiff here. The servants were terrified when we entered but gladly showed us the secret passage to your torture chamber."

The Count waved his hand around the room just as the bailiff's men returned.

"We have found more girls in another room deeper under the castle," said one of them breathlessly.

The bailiff left with his men but first sent for the doctor. "Lock all these animals up," he said to three of his men. "Take them out of here."

At the trial, which Countess Bathory never attended, the judge condemned all her accomplices to death. "Their guilt," he said in a passionate speech, "surpasses all evil and cruelty, and we, the Court of the Lord Palatine, and his Majesty King Matthias, sentence these murderers to burn."

And that is just what happened to Dorka, Janos, and Ficzko, as well as three other accomplices of Countess Bathory.

Count Thurzo, in an attempt to avoid a public execution of his cousin where all the facts would be made public, convinced the King to let him mete out justice to Countess Bathory.

The Countess had been kept prisoner during the trial in Csejthe Castle. When the verdict was in, Count Thurzo went there with Pastor Poniken and told her what had been decided. She would be stoned in, sealed in a room within the castle.

The Count, who was a tall, thin man, towered

over Countess Bathory. For once in her life she was silent. She knew she was beaten.

"Because of our family name I cannot have all your crimes made public," the Count said to her as she stood alone in the small room beyond where he and the pastor watched the plasterer work. "But you, Elisabeth, are like a wild animal and I cannot let you go free. You do not deserve to breathe the air on earth, or ever again to see the light of the Lord."

The stonemason had finished bricking in the windows of the small room and came out to start on the doorway.

The Count watched his cousin coldly. He had nothing but contempt for her. "You shall disappear from this world and shall never reappear in it again. The shadows will envelop you and you will find time to repent your bestial life. I condemn you, Lady Elisabeth of Csejthe, to lifelong imprisonment in your own castle. You will be sealed in a room, bricked in with only a small hole for food, and you will never be allowed to speak to or deal with another living being. You are in the last months of your life."

During this speech the mason had been working rapidly, and soon the last bricks sealing off the door were in place. Elisabeth stared wide-eyed and white-faced out of the small, remaining hole. She was too proud to plead, but fear filled her eyes. To die old and alone. She shuddered.

Acknowledgments

"The Green-Haired Giant of China" is an ancient legend from China about a vampire giant. However, in the tale there is no mention of drinking blood, so I have left out the vampire aspect. Freely adapted from *True Vampires of History,* by Donald Glut (New York: HC Publishers, Inc., 1971).

"The Demon Gebroo" is a tale about animal spirits that possess human beings. It is particularly common in Africa, which is where this legend comes from. This is a freely adapted tale from *Human Animals,* by Frank Hamel (London: William Rider & Son, Ltd., 1915).

"The Monster of Croglin Grange" is a famous legend in England, although little known outside its borders. It is freely adapted from *Haunted House,* by Charles Harper (n.p., 1924), and *Story of My Life,* by Augustus Hare, but mostly from *The Vampire in Europe,* by Montague Summers (London: Routledge & Kegan Paul, 1929).

"The Painted Skin" and "Black Magic" are two legends taken from *Strange Stories From a Chinese Studio*, by P'u Sung-ling, translated by Herbert Giles (London: Thomas de la Rue, 1880).

"The Legend of the Beautiful Werewolf" is adapted from the eighteenth-century book by French scholar Jules Michelet, *The Sorceress, A Study in Middle Age Superstition* (Paris: Charles Carrington, 1904), pp. 144–45.

"The Golem" is an ancient Jewish myth popular in Europe from the fifteenth century. There have been numerous retellings of the tale and some even feel that the Frankenstein story derived from the Golem idea. This version of the Golem legend uses only the magic ten words and the *emeth* paper that instills life from the original Polish text. The rest of the story is an amalgam of several different tales. My main source for the facts of the legend come from *The Golem of Prague* by Gershon Winkler, (New York: The Judaica Press, 1980). The tale however is freely adapted.

"The Murdering Ghost of London" is an old legend adapted from *Beyond Belief, Tales of the Supernatural*, by Stefan Elg (New York: Tower Books, 1967).

There are many tales and legends about monsters and giants in America's north woods. Various tribes call these hairy monsters by different names. In Oregon the Indians call these creatures "Oo-mah," or Big-foot. Others call them "Dsonoqua." In Washington the Indians call them "Sasquatch," or timber giant. "The Cannibal Giant Oo-mah" is adapted from a Kwakiutl myth of the British Columbian Indians, related in *Indian Masks and Myths of the West*, by Joseph Wherry (New York: Bonanza Books, 1968).

"The Burr Woman" is an American Indian myth about an old hag who attaches herself forever to the backs of people. This is almost the total myth, with different tribes having their own variations. There is no literary authority other than reference books on Indian folklore and myths where the Burr Woman is mentioned. I have used the basic idea but created the story line.

The same is true of this American Indian legend as with the Burr Woman. "The Windigo" is a legend to be found in folklore and myth references but whose story is simple: A group of Indians become lost in the forest and fall to eating each other to survive. The last survivor becomes a Windigo, a flesh-eating monster that roams the woods looking for lost people to feed on. Again, I have used this simple legend and embellished it with my own story line.

"The Snake Woman of Wales" was freely adapted from a Welsh folk legend reported in *Folklore and Folk Stories of Wales*, by Marie Trevelyan (n.p., 1909).

"Nevillon's Toad" is a traditional myth in Central Europe folklore. It is a simple story of a man who makes a puppet toad who bangs the floor every time he is hidden there by his maker. References to Nevillon's toad and this short tale can be found in many folklore reference books. I have adapted the tale freely and developed the story line.

"The Beast of Csejthe Castle" is based on the true story of the Countess Elisabeth Bathory, one of the most beastly humans to ever live. Much of the tale is fictionalized, but the facts are accurate and the events really happened.

The facts are taken from the trial record of 1611 when Elisabeth and her accomplices were convicted. Count Thurzo, the province's "Palatine" and Prime Minister of Hungary, was Elisabeth's cousin and presided at her trial. He succeeded in preventing her from being publicly executed for her crimes in order to protect the family name. His final speech to her as she is being sealed up in the prison room is accurate and his words are part of the court record. I have left the speech much as he spoke it.

I have remained as true to the actual facts as I could. In fact, her bloody life is so bestial that I couldn't relate all the gory details in their fullness.

The tale is adapted from two primary sources in which the trial records were translated: *The Truth About Dracula*, by Gabriel Ronay (New York: Scarborough House/Stein & Day, 1972) and *True Vampires of History*, by D. F. Glut (New York: HC Publishers, Inc., 1971).